THE SURGEON'S WIFE

The Surgeon's Wife

by
William H. Coles

Third edition

Published Aug, 2016

Story in Literary Fiction
Salt Lake City, Utah 84101

www.storyinliteraryfiction.com
facebook.com/storyinliteraryfiction

Cover art and illustrations by Betty Harper

ISBN: 978-0-9976729-4-7 (softcover)
ISBN: 978-0-9976729-5-4 (hardcover)
ISBN: 978-0-9976729-6-1 (ebook)

⚜ PART ONE ⚜

CHAPTER 1

M ike Boudreaux's gloved hands worked quickly and decisively to finish a gallbladder in operating room five. Paul Smythe, the anesthesiologist, entered from the corridor through swinging double doors. "Trouble in seven," he said, his usually calm voice edged with urgency.

Boudreaux's hands didn't hesitate in the measured motions of the instrument tie. The toothed forceps gripped the tissue, and with a twist of the needle holder, the needle passed cleanly through with little resistance. "Who is it?" he asked Paul, without taking his eyes off the field.

"Clayton."

"He ask for me?" Boudreaux asked.

Paul refused to answer a trivial question. He stared directly until Boudreaux met his gaze, and then he glanced in the direction of room seven to indicate the urgency.

Boudreaux finished one more tie and handed the instruments to the resident assistant. In seconds, he was in room seven. Except for the respirator and monitors, the room was silent. Clayton was bent over the OR table, his usual ruddy complexion now pale below the line of the blue surgical cap. The circulator stared at the floor, avoiding eye contact, her body slack from vexation and chagrin.

"Suction," Clayton said with a tenuous voice. The scrub nurse passed the instrument with a hesitant, uncertain motion, sweat beading on his forehead. Clayton pressed a sponge up into the wound, pulled it away, then activated the suction. The resident gripped the retractors with a fine tremor that faintly rippled the tissue held by the blade, his anxious eyes diverted from the field.

Boudreaux moved to the table and the assistant shifted toward the foot of the table to give him room to see without breaking sterility. He couldn't see any anatomy with the blood; a vessel had been cut. They needed better exposure.

There was no time to rescrub. From sterile packages the circulator dropped gown and gloves on a back table. Mike gowned and regloved, waiting for a look from Clayton. But Clayton worked mechanically with his eyes down, refusing to acknowledge Mike's presence. This was Clayton Otherson, his professor and mentor during training, nationally prominent for his bold innovations and unmatched results for so many years, his senior partner for the last twelve years, now floundering in indecision, unable to find the right choices to save his patient's life. Unthinkable.

The anesthetist, her face frustrated and angry, turned the monitor so he could see. The pulse was 138.

"I think I got it," Clayton mumbled.

Denial. The most dangerous response of the impaired physician.

"More blood's coming," Paul said directly to Mike, making adjustments to an IV, his gaze intent and away from Clayton.

With a firm nudge of his elbow, Mike moved the resident farther away from the action to gain a better view and access to expose the error. Clayton glared at him for the first time with red, rheumy eyes with a mixture of fear and humiliation.

Mike repositioned the retractors in the resident's hands, opening the abdominal wall incision by three inches. Emerging thick layers of fat gleamed above pools of arterial blood that had lost its healthy hue. Suction and irrigation isolated the artery that was cut through. With a tie, Mike stopped the bleeding.

He could feel Clayton's humiliation, the humiliation of needing help that eroded confidence and self-image, and that would never fade. But this was no time for sympathy. Clayton was in no condition to continue, and with his eyes Mike indicated to the resident to act as assistant from his position, without making Clayton move away from the table, to let him preserve some dignity.

With the bleeding sources stopped and the field dry, Mike finished the repair and started closure. Clayton left the table to take off his gown and leaned against a back wall, his head down. The anesthetist turned a stopcock on an IV line and adjusted gas flow percentages. She glanced at Mike with relief. The monitors changed pace slightly. As the resident completed the last sutures, he waited to be sure the blood pressure was safe, then told the resident to remove the drapes and dress the incision.

"I'll dictate," Clayton said to the resident, without looking at Mike.

Clayton yearned to turn back the clock, to be in control again. Mike paused before leaving but there was nothing he could say to comfort Clayton, and he hurried out of the room.

At seven o'clock that evening on the administrative floor, Mike looked up as his office door opened without a knock. Paul Smythe, the anesthesiologist, handed him a folder with four stapled sheets of paper.

"It's an incident report," Paul said. "On Otherson."

"Take it to Pat or Margaret, Paul," Mike said. Paul looked worried and angry.

"Read the goddamn report, Mike. I don't want any errors."

The report detailed Clayton's morning case. He looked up when he finished.

"Is this really necessary?"

"He's impaired, Boudreaux. If you see something I've written that's not right, change it."

"You can't know he's impaired, Paul. One case is not a trend. And it's a tricky label to put on any surgeon."

"This is not the first. I've seen other cases of his that have gone wrong. He doesn't know he's in trouble, and then he freezes."

"He's the best there is. I've spent a career trying to achieve what he has."

"*Was* the best. He's dangerous, Boudreaux. I don't know exactly why, but he needs to take a break."

Mike stood. "Hold the report," he said. "I'll talk to him. And investigate if there's a problem."

Paul stared defiantly. "That's not the way I'm going to handle this," he said. He did not like Clayton, nor most surgeons for that matter, and he thought Clayton's privileges should be suspended based on poor performance. But Mike knew this was not personal for Paul. Paul cared about his patients . . . not just his reputation. He was among the best in his specialty.

Paul took back the pages. "Don't try to bury this, Boudreaux," he said.

Mike glared. "I'm not your problem, Paul. Stay civil."

"You're chief of service with the duty to act. And don't delay."

"I'm not dishonest, Paul. I'll do what needs to be done."

Paul frowned and shook his head slowly. "I misspoke," he said. "You'll do what's right. But he needs to step down . . . and I don't see him doing it on his own."

CHAPTER 2

The rain slapped sheets across the windshield, blurring the yellow glow of the streetlights. Mike heard the clang of a St. Charles streetcar on the median less than a hundred feet from the street, but could not see it in the night darkness.

This was upscale New Orleans, where blocks of multimillion-dollar houses – most unfriendly and pretentious – hunkered among surrounding sections of third-world-style poverty shacks teeming with angry, sick people. He'd long ago started to refuse the stand-up parties – those that involved leaning on hundred-thousand-dollar grand pianos while Mozart or Chopin was expertly, if not loudly, rendered. These were archaic, lifeless caves, excessive living space with echoes. Hell yes, he was jealous, too. The owners had generations of family wealth that he had never had. And they shunned him socially for his lack of aristocratic heritage. He couldn't help being born poor. It would make more sense, and irritate him less, if these aristocrats turned him away because his breath reeked. Well, maybe their self-perceived splendor was what money did to the soul. He never believed he'd wanted that. Of course it was a rationalization. He'd never had the opportunity to give it a try. He was Cajun, brought up by his mother, worked his way through school next to the privileged, so he was never accepted as one of them. And he believed at times that it was his hard work to grow and thrive in spite of his background that had made him the best surgeon in the state, chief of surgery at the third largest hospital in the country. He'd done it, goddamn it, without the contacts of the upper echelons of New Orleans society. Except, of course, for Clayton. His teacher, his mentor. Clayton guided his promotions and appointments. Professionally, not socially. In the world of surgery. He owed Clayton a lot – at the least, sympathy and guidance that might save Clayton's career.

He pulled into the drive of Clayton's turn-of-the-twentieth-century stone house. It had been more than a year since he'd been here. There were sixteen surgeons on service, and, except for department and university functions, Mike never socialized with his colleagues unless absolutely necessary, even after he was appointed chief four years ago.

A lightning flash illuminated the huge live oak in the front yard as he pulled his car under a small portico at the rear of the house to avoid the roof runoff. In the rain-slashed glare of a single spotlight, the wind whipped the banana leaves at the edge of the house. Clayton would probably be in the modern add-on solarium at the rear. The floodlight over the back door was dark, and Mike felt for the bell button and rang.

Catherine, Clayton's wife, answered. He peered into her wary eyes. He wondered how much she knew. She was two or three years younger than Mike, and more than twenty-five years younger than Clayton. Mike could not imagine Clayton discussing the details of his daily work with her. And to him she'd been pleasant, but distant, always aloof, giving a sense of perpetual subconscious eagerness to be elsewhere. Mike had seen her a few times in the last couple of years, just to say hello in a grocery store, or on the street when she was with Clayton during Mardi Gras or the Jazz Festival.

"Clayton in?" he asked. She stood back and he entered.

She wore a gray workout suit with white side-stripes. Her black hair was in a ponytail, and in the weak ambient light that filtered in from the dining room her face was unusually pale; she wore no makeup. He had always found her attractive, and even in workout clothes she had an elegance he admired.

"Why are you out in this?" she asked without greeting.

"It's about work."

"That's what it's always about." She looked away. "He's in the solarium."

She didn't move as he walked from the kitchen through the old portion of the house – the foyer, the dining room with seating for twelve, a hall – all restored and filled with museum-quality, antique

Louisiana and European furniture – and then he stepped down through the double doors of the two-story solarium, a lush jungle of hanging and potted plants, vines, trees, and blooms. Clayton's bottomless-well family money had allowed Catherine – obviously an exceptional horticulturist – to create a showcase of beautiful specimens. She was the pride of her garden group, Mike was sure.

In the solarium, Clayton sat on a sofa with his feet up on an ottoman. He had on a fluffy cotton robe with only his undershorts below, but still wore his white shirt and rep tie from the day. He gathered the front of his robe together.

"Michael!"

"Yes, sir," Mike said. He regretted the "sir" under the circumstances. It was habit. He couldn't shake the tradition of respect for the guys above you who had decades of experience, although technically, as chief of service, he was now Clayton's boss.

Clayton picked up a remote and fumbled for the button to cut off the giant-screen TV. He paused. The fourth hurricane of the year was in the Gulf. Red circles next to dotted and solid lines covered the full-screen map. A commercial came on. Clayton clicked and the picture faded.

"You're looking bushed, Mike. You're working too hard." He waved a hand. "Sit down."

Mike moved past Clayton, who studied a hanging spider plant dangling on a long chain from a ceiling hook thirty feet above, and sat on the edge of a white wicker sofa.

"It's about today," Mike said. "Paul's filed an incident report."

"Bury it, Mike."

Catherine came in with a coffeepot and slices of lemon pound cake on a silver serving tray. Her hair was down and brushed now, shining with highlights. Her lips glinted with fresh lipstick.

"Leave us for a few minutes, baby," Clayton said.

Catherine poured coffee for each of them and left, her silent steps almost ghostly in the damp shadows of the plants. She didn't react to her dismissal. Being excluded didn't seem to bother her.

Clayton leaned forward and sipped from a cup.

"I've been around for a long time, Mike. I don't deserve this shit.

Make that report disappear."

Mike shook his head. "It's not internal, Clayton. It's gone up the ladder. I can't stop it."

"If it goes to the OR committee, we'll be out of control," Clayton said.

"It's out of my control now. It comes from anesthesia."

"Jesus, man. I know Paul likes you. Talk to him. Make him see the light."

"He's concerned, Clayton." Mostly for the patients. But he also didn't like the way Clayton's practice had shifted to the obese. Paul felt the surgery had high risks and questionable benefits.

"He's not a surgeon, Mike. He shouldn't be making judgments on us."

"He's a damned good anesthesiologist. And he cares for you. Honestly, he thinks as I do. If you step down, this would never get to the OR committee for action."

"Why would I step down?"

"Cut back, then."

"The bypass stuff is growing, Mike. Obesity is pandemic. It's no time to cut back."

"Do the obese surgery without laparoscopy. It's the laps that are getting you in trouble."

Clayton leaned back in his chair and closed his eyes. Mike waited.

"I'm not wrong here," Clayton said. "I'm the best. One little mistake doesn't change that."

"No one's better than you. But you've got to catch up on the new techniques."

"Is that as friend or chief of service?"

"Both."

"I've done a lot for this department."

"And for surgery worldwide," Mike added.

"I don't deserve this shit."

"Paul tells me you've had other problems."

Clayton thought for a moment. "For Christ's sake. It's temporary. Every surgeon has ups and downs. You know that," he said.

"It won't fly."

"I can't cancel cases, Mike. I'm booked for months. I might lose my block time if I take time off."

Mike stared at his untouched coffee. "Telling the committee won't be enough. They'll be under a strong moral imperative when it comes to patient safety."

"I bring in a lot of cases, Mike. I damn near support this department."

"It's got nothing to do with how many cases you have," he said. "You made a mistake, Clayton."

"I'm telling you. It could happen to anyone."

"No, Clayton. It did not happen to anyone. Face facts. It would not happen to very many. And it should never happen here again."

Clayton made a wet hiss with his mouth. "I didn't need you today!" he said.

"She could have died!"

"You overreacted. You like the glory."

Mike stood in anger.

Clayton called over his shoulder toward the kitchen. "Honey. Bring Mike a drink. He's upset." Then he looked at Mike. "Sit down."

Mike lowered himself back into the chair.

"Listen up. I'm not stepping down," Clayton said. "I'll do the training stuff, but I'm not stepping down."

Clayton turned on the TV with the remote. Mike shrugged. "I think that's a mistake."

"Make it right, then. Bury that report. You owe me," Clayton said. "You want your drink?"

"Nothing for me."

Mike knew Catherine was close by, and that she had listened to every word. But she stayed hidden. He let himself out.

Catherine had listened to every word from the dining room. She slipped into the hall when Mike left. She walked back into the kitchen after the door closed and leaned forward with her hands on the counter, her head down.

"Catherine!" Clayton called.

Clayton was becoming impossible. Irritated, unreasonable. He had paranoid fears about the world coming after him and seemed close to striking out against anyone or anything that was close by, especially her and his friends who cared. And now this. A failure that would only make him worse.

"I'm going out," she said.

"Where?"

"To talk to Mike."

"It's nothing to do with you. Keep out of it, Catherine."

"I'll be back in a few minutes," she said.

In his car, with the key in the ignition, Mike paused, resting his forehead on the steering wheel. He had failed. How could he have done it better? Catherine knocked on the window.

"Let me in. I'm wet."

He hesitated, a sense of dread seizing him. Then he undid the locks.

Catherine climbed in and closed the door. She crossed her arms, her hands gripping her shoulders. She was shivering. She was silent for more than a moment.

"You heard?" he asked.

"Of course I heard, Michael. I was in the kitchen fixing drinks."

He stared ahead. "It's serious. He's got to realize it's serious. They're labeling him impaired."

"It's you."

"Not me, Catherine."

"You took over his case."

"The anesthesiologist thought she was going to die on the table. She was right."

"You'll destroy him. You, especially. He's loved you like a son, Michael. From the day you came on service."

The words hurt him. "I failed to convince him to do what's best for him. That's what I had to do. But I've let him down."

"You're the chief of service. He believes you're the one who will take away his privileges."

"Never. If it comes to that, it will be the OR committee."

"You're the chair of that committee."

"Without the power to make them go against what they will believe is wrong. He is wrong. And they'll all believe it."

"What's wrong?"

"To let him keep operating when he's dangerous."

She turned her head to look at him for the first time. "How can you say that?"

"He's doing a lot of bariatric surgery and he's using the laparoscope, Catherine. He has not trained and he's not adapted well."

"Help him."

"I don't do much of the obese stuff."

"Help him learn laparoscopy."

"I can't get him to agree. He won't listen to me."

She looked away and sighed. "He's so arrogant sometimes."

"It's pride, Catherine. Much of the time it's well-deserved pride."

"Well, don't let him fail. He deserves that from you after all these years."

He shook his head. "You can encourage him to step down. Just for a few weeks. Call it a vacation. Go on a retreat or something."

"He never listens to me, Michael. I'm a wife, not a colleague. And I haven't been confident enough around him to be blunt. For years."

"If he won't step down, I promise, we'll watch him carefully. All the staff. We all want to get him through this."

"And the incident report?"

"There's nothing I can do. It's gone too far."

She opened the door and turned as she got out as if she were going to say something. But she shut the door, and he watched her walk slowly in the rain to the house, her movements tentative, as if she dreaded entering again.

CHAPTER 3

Two weeks later, Mike left the chilled, filtered air of an operating room, lowered his surgical mask as he walked down the humid hall, and went into the dressing room. He took a white lab coat from the hook in his locker and retrieved his wallet and keys from the upper shelf. He pulled his lab coat on over his green scrubs and walked to the elevator.

Four minutes later he was on the twelfth floor. He opened the door to the administrative conference room.

Around the long, oval oak table in straight-backed wooden chairs sat the members of the hospital OR committee: nine surgeons, each representing a department; an OR coordinator; a secretary for minutes; an assistant dean; and the chair of anesthesia. He sat in the only empty chair, left vacant for him as the chair of the committee and chief of surgery. He never thought to apologize for his lateness; he was often late, but, as all the others knew, it wasn't because he was lazy or slow. His time was never his own. No one in the room, friend or foe, blamed him. He nodded to the secretary, who started a tape recorder.

He followed the agenda: minutes approved, a vote on a new tech position, approval of a staged renovation of recovery room C, all thirteen items above five thousand dollars approved for purchase, financial stats since December reviewed. He could feel the unusual tension in the room. If he could delay consideration of Paul's report on Clayton until the next meeting, he might fix Clayton's problems and lessen the severity of the committee action. He was about to close the meeting.

Janet from orthopedics stood up demanding attention for new

business. She was the first one to stand since the beginning of the meeting. He'd seen her memos about surgery for the obese. She was on a crusade against surgery for weight loss, and even though Clayton's technical mistake was not directly related to obesity, it happened during a procedure for weight control and was exactly the ammunition she needed to load her gun for lethal shots against the surgeons. "You can sit down," Mike said.

She ignored him. "Each of you has read my risk management memo. Each of you knows about this OR error of Otherson's." She paused. "A life-threatening complication of a gastric bypass! Bleeding out. Otherson should have his privileges rescinded."

"A report has been filed," Mike said. "It needs to come through channels."

"We have responsibilities to make corrections now," Janet said.

"The patient has no permanent damage," a general surgeon said. "You just don't like the operation."

"It's Otherson," she said with a controlled voice. "Making advertising claims that can't be true. Operating on anything that walks in the door. Threatening the life of a patient."

"I don't understand," Oral Surgery said.

"You're a fucking dentist," Janet replied.

"I'm dual trained." He shrugged his shoulders and looked around the table for support. No one responded.

"It's the bypass surgery. They're . . ." Janet stared at Mike. ". . . on television, and radio."

"It's common practice everywhere," said another general surgeon.

"Make your point, Janet," Mike said.

"There's a national backlash against the procedure and now we're advertising. It makes no sense. It's become elective surgery and a patient in our hospital damn near died. Stop Otherson now!"

"Be reasonable," said Thoracic.

"Don't suggest I'm unreasonable because I'm the only one to bring to this committee what everyone knows. It's not a good treatment. And it's expensive. And it almost killed someone. And if I hadn't brought it up, every one of you would have been happy to let it pass."

"Not me," said Oral Surgery.

"Please sit down, Janet . . ." Mike began.

"I don't want to sit down!"

"I was there. The complication was laparoscopic, and had nothing to do with gastric bypass."

"She wouldn't have been on the table if she hadn't signed a consent for bypass surgery. She expected weight loss. She almost lost her life."

Janet's point was valid, but her remedies were off the mark and too severe. He was losing tolerance. "If indications for bypass surgery are a problem, Janet, we'll deal with that separately. The report is about a single complication. I've talked to Otherson. He's agreed to more training with laparoscopy."

"And he'll stop operating?"

"He's agreed to do open procedures until he's finished with the training on laparoscopic surgery."

Janet looked around the table. "That is not satisfactory. I move to revoke privileges to operate."

Mike waited.

"Second," said ENT.

"Call the question," Thoracic said.

Mike allowed for discussion. The room was silent. Janet had stirred up a mood of hostility among the surgeons that discouraged supporting her on any issue. He pressed on.

"All in favor," he began. Two ayes. Seven nays.

"Motion is defeated." Clayton was saved from any immediate surgical restrictions on operations for obesity. His technical improvement using laparoscopy would be his own responsibility through attending training from national experts.

Janet sat. "It still doesn't address the advertising. He's promising more than can be expected."

She wouldn't let go. It was her need for confrontation – against everything, not just Clayton or surgeons. "We've voted," Mike said. "That's an issue for the next meeting."

"Morbid obesity is a nationwide problem and growing," Oral Surgery said immediately, to prevent a motion to adjourn. "We have to deal with it!"

"What do you know about it?" a general surgeon snapped. "Fucking dentist," he mumbled, but all heard.

Janet grinned and nodded. "He knows what I know . . . and that's a hell of a lot!"

"I'm on the ethics committee," Ophthalmology said. "There's concern. He's operating with a very low threshold for indications."

"Don't be trivial," the general surgeon said.

"Morbid obesity is hardly trivial," Ophthalmology countered.

"That's why we operate, you idiot," the general surgeon said.

"A lot of well-founded suspicions of preventable complications caused by bariatric surgery are simmering in every clinic in this hospital."

"It's reasonable to find facts," Mike said. "We'll check the results. It will be a top agenda item as soon as possible."

"That's not enough," said Oral Surgery. "I move Otherson at least be censured for bariatrics. That would give the hospital some legal protection."

"It's insulting," Thoracic said.

"It's only a slap on the wrist," Janet said.

"Second," Ophthalmology said. "It'll tell him we're watching. And that we expect him to curb obese surgery in addition to retraining."

"Is that what you want to do? A formal censure?" Mike asked the committee.

On vote, only two of the general surgeons and Thoracic disagreed.

As the meeting adjourned, Mike whispered to the coordinator to have Otherson's obese stats on his desk tomorrow afternoon.

He went to his office and called Clayton directly. "You were censured."

"What the fuck does that mean?"

"You'll be informed in writing that the committee does not approve of your low threshold for recommending bariatric surgery. But if you tighten your indications, you can operate."

"Without restrictions on other surgeries?"

"Only restrictions on use of the laparoscope. They agree with the additional training in laps. Just reevaluate your indications for obese surgery."

"You should have done more," Clayton said.

"You should have stepped down," Mike said and hung up.

The next afternoon Mike received the coordinator in his office. She laid a report on his desk.

"Sit down," he said. He studied the report.

As part of the general surgery service, gastric bypass surgery was expanding rapidly. Obese was a financial success.

The bulk of the report was devoted to outcomes. Department bariatric mortality was higher than the published national average by almost two percent, significant at the .01 level. Clayton would argue the cases done were often the most difficult, and that a case mix weighted with seriously ill patients would always increase the mortality. But it was clear, too, that the body mass index threshold had been lowered so that the concept of morbid obesity had changed. In essence, skinnier people were now being offered the operation based on lowered admission criteria.

"Where is patient satisfaction?" Mike asked the coordinator.

"There's not much," she said. "I put what I could find in the appendix."

"Any significant findings?"

"Hard to quantitate the quality-of-life stuff. But look at the summary page. The research protocols for studying psychological adjustment don't meet the standards of other institutions, and the results we have are below standards."

"It doesn't look good," he said mostly to himself.

"One third had no effective weight loss. Those who did lose weight had a recurrence rate of more than fifty percent. One hundred percent are on lifetime vitamins and supplements."

"We're being accused of operating for cash and lowering the indications," he said. "What do you think?"

"I wouldn't have the operation," she said. "Even if I dove into a swimming pool and emptied all the water out."

"Sit on these stats until the meeting."

"I'm not a crusader," she said. "Whistleblowers are the first ones pushed out a top-story window."

"But you don't like what you see?"

"I'm ashamed. It's got nothing to do with the profession of healing."

Within minutes Mike was in the office of Hammond McLaughlin, the chair of the department of surgery, who was a head shorter than he even when they were sitting. McLaughlin had a new red scaly patch on his head near the front. It needed treatment.

McLaughlin took out a comb and gave his bald dome a self-conscious left-to-right comb-over.

"Make it snappy, Mike. I've got an interview waiting."

Mike laid the report on McLaughlin's desk. "You need to give this some thought, Hammond."

"Clayton warned me. Said you might be coming by."

"We've slipped," Mike said. "We're doing borderline cases. Some unnecessary."

"Speak straight, Mike. It's not 'we.' It's Clayton you're after."

"He does more than ninety percent of the surgeries."

McLaughlin pushed back from his desk. "You're accusing Clayton?"

"Not accusing. We need tighter indications for all surgeons."

McLaughlin turned serious. "Jesus, Mike. He's a good man. We went to school together. I was in his wedding . . . did you know that? I flew in from Philadelphia. Stayed at his mother's place – like some fucking castle for a queen. Filthy rich."

"It's not just Clayton," Mike said, exasperated. "There are others starting up. We need department-wide rules. I've reviewed his bariatric cases – his indications are loose. On his volume alone, the bad outcomes add up fast."

"Don't make this personal, Mike. This 'we all need tighter indications' is a lot of crap. This is about Clayton making a mistake. We all accept he made a mistake."

"It's not personal!" Mike said. "And he makes mistakes on his bariatric cases." McLaughlin assumed everyone acted in his own interest. "He was my mentor," Mike added. "This is not easy for me."

"Then back off. Clayton is the number one surgeon in gross billings and collections. He damn near supports this department.

All the start-up guys' salaries depend on him. And all those no-pay surgeries you like to do. Those trauma cases from out of state? Not possible without support from faculty like Clayton!"

"It can't be money, Hammond. That's not what we're about."

"Don't be an idiot. It's all about money. The state keeps cutting back. Medicare and Medicaid deny and won't pay a reasonable percentage. Money keeps us afloat. That's life. Guys like Clayton save guys like you; it's like some shitty socialistic mandate."

Mike took a straight-back chair and dragged it near the desk to sit in front of McLaughlin. "Listen carefully," Mike said. "A majority of the OR committee is very concerned over this bariatric issue. And the technical failure, too. Orthopedics will turn this into a battle against surgery that will up their power in the OR. And they've got a silver-bullet issue here. Believe me, this is not the time to dodge and weave."

McLaughlin frowned. "Clayton doesn't deserve this," he said and picked up the report, tilting his head to focus his reading glasses. He scanned it just enough to shiver with a shard of fear over the potential damage it contained.

Mike stared. Hammond played favorites. His best skill was politics. He avoided conflicts and rarely made decisions unless pressed. But most disturbing, he resented the good surgeons, resented what they could do, what he would never achieve in the OR. He had built his shaky power base in administration to find some value in his career.

"Can this report be trusted?" McLaughlin asked.

Mike tensed. "Nothing is faked. I'm chair of the OR committee. I don't make up bad outcomes."

McLaughlin tilted back in his chair. He wasn't finished talking. "We can't restrict our faculty," he said thoughtfully. "We hire a guy like Clayton, he comes to do his thing. He's honest, trying to do the best he can. Volume is important. He ought to have the right to choose his cases."

Mike leaned forward. "Clayton's advertising. Orthopedics is right to be upset. The marketers fake pre-op shots using actors with pillows stuffed in their clothes, then cut to fake post-ops with the same guy strutting fatless on a beach in a Speedo. That's not helping the sick, that's looking for people who will agree to a risky operation."

"That's unfair ..."

"Fair is exactly how most of the OR committee sees it. They might let Clayton operate after a lap bleed-out, but they didn't like that it was obese elective surgery."

Mike made an effort to keep his voice normal. He took the report from McLaughlin and stood.

"This was gathered by the committee coordinator. It will be committee information. Unless you take action, the committee will take action. It will be common knowledge. The world will come down on us."

"Calm down." McLaughlin paused. "Look. I see your point."

"I need action. Not understanding."

"I'll call a task force. That's the way to handle it. That way all sides can be heard."

"This is not a sporting event, Hammond. The department needs to publish strict indications."

McLaughlin looked up at him. "A task force is action. No one could fault that."

"We're trying to improve patient care, not escape fault."

"Patient care issues need a measured, non-emotional approach." Hammond wrote names on a pad. "Use these names. They're our friends; you choose more if you need to."

"The task force will have more clout if the names come directly from you," Mike said.

"You're the one with a carrot up your ass."

As Mike walked out, he gave a full list of names to McLaughlin's administrative assistant to make the arrangements for the first task force meeting. He had little respect for McLaughlin's delaying tactics. It could take months to work this out, for better or for worse.

CHAPTER 4

Rosemary Dayside stood with Mike among their suitcases and looked out the picture window of their hotel suite. The river was hidden by the levee some two hundred yards away, but the top half of a tanker was visible as it glided by. She savored the colors of the end-of-April flowers that lined the walkways to the river, glowing in the late afternoon sun. The hotel was part of a renovated plantation resort project downriver from Baton Rouge that, because of its convention facilities, had been a favorite choice for the annual faculty retreat for some years.

The sky had a few threatening late-day clouds to the south near the horizon. It would be a shame if storms spoiled the open-air social events. She'd brought delicate fair-weather outfits – colorful, revealing, demure. She had planned carefully to divert attention from her working-class origins. She busied herself hanging things in the walk-in closet and taking items from her suitcase to dresser drawers under a built-in TV set.

Mike sat down in an overstuffed chair and stretched his legs. She prepared to shower, hiding herself from his direct view. Even after two years of dating she still felt shy undressing in front of him. It was part of her family belief. Single women – well, she was divorced – but, she still had certain modesty standards.

"What's tonight?" she asked as she dried herself with a bath towel.

"Cocktails at six, dinner at seven."

She slipped into the walk-in closet and unzipped a hanging garment bag while watching him unpack his tuxedo, old enough to have a worn sheen on the elbows. He held it up to look for wrinkles.

She moaned. "I thought this was resort-casual tonight. I brought only short dresses." She held up one black and one red dress from her bag and then replaced them.

"It won't make any difference," he said.

It made a big difference; it was demeaning to be inappropriate.

"I'll need hose . . ." she said softly to herself. She picked up her over-the-shoulder bag near Mike's chair. Mike said nothing.

When she was in the hall, she closed the door quietly. He must be thinking about something important.

In the gift shop, she stood at the checkout counter.

"We're out," said the clerk. "Maybe the middle of next week."

"I have a formal dinner tonight. Is there someplace else?"

"There's a Walmart toward Lafayette."

"How long would that take?"

"Thirty minutes round-trip. Maybe forty."

A woman waited behind her to purchase a bottle of wine. "Are you with the faculty?" the woman asked.

"I'm Michael Boudreaux's date. He's a surgeon."

"Michael works with my husband, Clayton Otherson. I'm Catherine Otherson."

"I'm Rosemary."

"Maybe I can help. I've got hose."

Catherine bought the wine and had it gift-wrapped. "For the vice president of clinical affairs," she explained.

The woman seemed pleasant enough, but there was a trace of curiosity in her look; maybe she was making a judgment about her as Mike Boudreaux's date. Well, no matter. She couldn't go bare-legged in a short dress to a formal dance. And the Otherson woman seemed willing enough to help.

In the narrow hall, she walked slightly behind Catherine to the Othersons' room. "I brought two short casual dresses," she explained.

"That would be fine anywhere else. But this is a pretentious bunch," Catherine said.

"Maybe I shouldn't go. Would it hurt Michael if I just bagged it?"

"I really don't know," Catherine said. She removed a key card from the pocket of her white linen slacks. Rosie took the package with the bottle of wine to free her hands. Catherine paused before inserting the card.

"We're about the same size," Catherine said looking at her. "I could lend you a dress."

Rosie was surprised. "Oh, no, really . . . I couldn't . . ."

"We drove and I threw dresses into the car. I had no idea what I wanted to wear. You might fit into one."

"What if you need it?"

"Don't be ridiculous. This will be fun."

Catherine called to Clayton. No one answered. "Good," she said, "He's in the bar politicking. He comes with a list of people he's got to convince of one thing or another."

In the bedroom, Catherine picked out a dress that fit Rosie perfectly – like a hand in a glove. Clothes were obviously important to Catherine, a statement of wealth and class.

"It's beautiful," Rosie said. The perfect tailoring made her feel alluring and elegant. "Are you sure it's okay?"

"You do it justice," Catherine smiled. "On me, it's not a favorite."

In her pleasure, Rosie gave Catherine a grateful embrace.

"I'm so pleased it fits," Catherine said.

Rosie went back to the room with the dress draped carefully over her arm.

"Hi," Mike said without looking up from the chair where he was reading.

She dressed out of his view, in the bedroom. "I met Catherine Otherson in the gift shop," she called to Mike.

"Did you like her?"

"From the start," she said. "She loaned me a long dress for the dance." As she adjusted the dress in front of the mirror, she flushed with pleasure.

Mike did not respond. Minutes later she touched his shoulder. She stood back and gave a twirl, her face radiant.

"You look wonderful," he said.

"You'll be proud of me?"

He stood and wrapped his arms around her. "You're the best."

The banquet room was airplane-hangar size, carpeted in deep red, with a thirty-five-foot domed ceiling. A raised bandstand with chairs for a twenty-piece orchestra was in place at one end, next to a stage with a long table for dignitaries and an oak podium for the speakers.

She felt the gazes of men as she walked to a reserved table, her arm interlocked with Michael's. To one side she saw Catherine in an off-the-shoulder pale-gray full-length gown with white trim that she had seen in her closet earlier. It seemed perfect for the evening. Catherine's shoulder-length black hair glinted with reflections from the room's seven-tiered crystal chandelier.

Mike led Rosie to a table where two other surgeons and their wives were seated. Catherine sat with Clayton at a dignitaries' table, and Rosie had no chance to talk to her. But she smiled when Catherine saw her, and felt an almost conspiratorial warmth when Catherine gave her an approving nod.

CHAPTER 5

The meetings started at eight o'clock the next morning.

Mike arrived late and sat on the aisle about halfway back of the five-hundred-seat auditorium. It was about half full. He'd left his program in the room, but he didn't go back for it. This was a plenary session and would have no information he needed to listen to intently.

The chancellor spoke. Throughout the bored, inattentive audience, heads nodded, half asleep or lost in private thoughts. A few read journals or corrected manuscripts. Others had open laptops. Mike himself wasn't so interested in what the chancellor was saying, but he didn't approve of rudeness from the faculty. He settled in to use the time effectively by mentally going over a possible new procedure for gallbladder removal.

The air warmed from the body heat of the crowd and insufficient ventilation, and he became aware that many minutes had passed; he had not tracked the time. He heard the Otherson name. He turned back to the chancellor, who was still speaking on the stage. They weren't speaking of Clayton Otherson, but Catherine Otherson. Strange. She wasn't a doctor, and not faculty. He saw movement near stage right. She must have been sitting in the front row. She wore a gray dress suit with a pale yellow blouse. She was compact and trim. She climbed up the stage stairs gracefully, with the controlled steps of an athlete, and walked to the podium. For the first time ever, he found her striking. She knew her worth as a woman. He'd not been around her enough over the years, when her role had been always as a hostess or as Clayton's devoted companion, to see it before. But here, on this stage, presenting to this group of arrogant cynics, her confidence was obvious and appealing.

He glanced over the crowd but didn't see Clayton.

The chancellor welcomed Mrs. Otherson's announcement. Clayton Otherson's devoted wife, he said. Clayton Otherson, professor of surgery, who was no stranger to anyone in this room. Not a word about Catherine's accomplishments. Mike cringed at the sexism, which was ubiquitous at these meetings.

Catherine showed no reaction to the blatantly inappropriate comments. Not that he had expected any. She was far too self-controlled to be flustered in public. He was surprised again, though, after the introduction, that nothing in her dignified presence showed a trace of kowtowing to this mainly male audience.

She thanked the chancellor for his introduction, her voice comfortable and polished. The psychic tone of the room shifted from near-dead to crisply attentive. Everyone now focused on Catherine, not because of her announcement, but because she was stunningly pleasant to look at.

She began. "I am pleased to announce that an unrestricted, two-million-dollar surgical endowed chair has been donated by Surgigen International. This company, a supplier of instruments and sutures to surgeons around the world, has chosen to recognize the University Hospital, and the department of surgery, with this generous gift to support the education of new surgeons." She used no notes. A recipient for a fellowship had been chosen and the honoree would be announced in the fall.

When she finished, the chancellor finally gave full credit to her as an active and talented fundraiser for the alumni association.

Two other dignitaries were called to present major donations to the university, but Catherine was the star. Catherine had revved up their fantasies. He smiled. She was not your everyday stay-at-home housewife; oddly, he found that her success had pleased him more than he would have expected.

Later that afternoon, Rosie climbed the tour bus steps in front of the hotel drive. Catherine sat at a window seat near the back.

"May I join you?" Rosie asked.

"Of course," Catherine said.

Rosie thanked Catherine again for the loan of the dress, and told her she had dropped it off at the concierge to be cleaned and delivered to their suite.

"How beautiful you looked last night," Rosie said.

Catherine smiled. "You too."

"Have you been on this tour before?" Rosie asked.

"I put it together. The bus is commercial, but the guide is a volunteer from the Historical Society. I'm on the board."

Cather's tone was matter of fact, not mean or suggesting irritation that Rosie did not know. Still, it brought back her insecurities that surfaced around the rich and successful. She longed to learn the leadership skills that seemed so natural to Catherine. But she'd never be comfortable directing people; she didn't like to chance an offense. Catherine had confidence that moved people without offending them; she could see that. Was it just money? Or genes? Or had someone taught her?

The bus drove by hundreds of acres of cane stalks, elephant high and sturdy. Through the built-in sound system, the tour guide talked about the cane industry.

"My husband, and Mike, too, treat all sorts of injuries to the cane workers," Catherine whispered to Rosie. "They get mangled in the machinery."

Catherine did not speak as they passed neatly kept, unpainted, slant-roof houses in small clusters near crossroads. The levee was to the right of the road. Occasional refineries or chemical plants jutted silo-shaped towers and chimneys into the air. Variously sized pipes, painted white, crisscrossed acres of flat land, bland and tan and dusty dry. The river was rarely visible, but occasionally the tops of bulk carriers glided by.

For many minutes Catherine did not look out the window, and kept her thoughts to herself. As they rode together, Rosie had come to like Catherine even more, and she could feel Catherine's morose silence – ominous, like a pre-hurricane calm.

Rosie worried now. Her nature was to blame herself for anything she possibly could. It frustrated her. It never made her feel better, but she couldn't help it. Why had Catherine's mood changed? Could it be something she'd said? Something too personal? Inappropriate? Rosie couldn't think of anything. Besides, Catherine seemed immune to slights; she was so talented, so admired – and before now she had seemed immune to melancholy.

"Can I help?" Rosie ventured after a few minutes.

Catherine did not reply.

When they exited the bus at the plantation, Catherine left the group to sit alone on a wrought-iron bench. Rosie went into the house, but after seeing a ballroom painted all white – even the floors and ceiling – and a dining room in white with a table set with French china and real silverware, she slipped away and went outside to enjoy the sun. Catherine was still on the bench. Rosie sat down beside her.

"I love that ballroom," Catherine said. "I've always hoped my daughter will be married there."

"Is she engaged?"

"She's seventeen. She has a boyfriend that she won't introduce to Clayton or me, but I hope she's too busy partying to fall in love."

"I think New Orleans is like that. I mean . . . too busy to fall in love."

"You're not from here?"

"North Carolina. But I've been here twenty years."

"You think falling in love is different in North Carolina?"

"I think New Orleans erodes family values."

"That seems a little harsh," said Catherine. "It's not easy to generalize. I guess you have only your own experiences."

Rosie needed to explain. She paused for words, feeling inadequate around this talented woman. "It's the 'city that care forgot.' There's truth to that in many ways. People seem not to care about each other. Like they forget others are around."

"And it's better in Carolina?"

"I grew up on a tobacco farm. I still carry concerns for my family and friends. I don't see those concerns very often in New Orleans."

Catherine stared off in the distance. Did she agree?

Catherine spoke after a pause. "Where's your family now? Do you have children?"

She pulled back. "I'm divorced." She knew it wasn't reasonable, but suddenly she didn't want to discuss her personal problems. Catherine's inexplicable sadness had changed their space. Meanings between them seemed different. And Catherine was prying with questions that hurt.

"Was that a failure of love New Orleans-style? Was he from New Orleans?"

She didn't want to begin the memories. "He was incapable of love."

"It's the curse of males."

She paused. "Not just men and love. I think it's lust in New Orleans. It's not love."

"Is that the way it is with Michael?" Catherine asked.

Rosie flinched. She loved Michael. And it was more than just lust. She had to be sure about that. But she wasn't sure that his love for her absolute, or all-consuming. He did want her. But could he do without her? That was what concerned her. She didn't fill his heart the way she wanted.

"That was rude," Catherine said. "I'm out of sorts."

"It wasn't rude," Rosie lied. Catherine was a woman who could make a man want her. She was, in so many ways, a Helen of Troy of New Orleans. Rosie wondered if Catherine could love any man the way she, Rosie, loved Michael.

"Sometimes I feel useless," Catherine said. "This plantation. A hollow, pretentious remnant of some arrogant plantation owner. Buried in life by his possessions and buried with the care of a friend, unremembered by anyone except for his selfish luxury in the sea of poverty that surrounded him – defined him, really," she said. "I think you're right about New Orleans not caring," she added.

"His house has given pleasure to many generations," Rosie said, her reply more reflexive than considered.

"I spoke with more curiosity than awe of the place," Catherine said.

"But you want your daughter to be married here."

"To fit into the heritage. Clayton's family goes back. I'm a Hebert and we're new by comparison. I want her to be a cornerstone of New Orleans. To make her future easier."

"You're already so successful as a family."

"It's a facade. I'm unfulfilled. It hits me sometimes. No one gives a damn." Catherine forced a smile. "But what about your family?"

"I guess I don't have much family anymore." In truth, she hadn't seen her family for more than a decade. Her brother had moved west when their parents died.

"Michael is your family?"

"Michael is too busy most of the time be family. It's his profession."

"But if he loves you . . ."

"He notices me when he's not at the hospital and when he's not exhausted," Rosie confessed. "How does your husband manage?"

"He's the same." Catherine said. "I'm married seventeen years, just out of Newcomb. I thought he could love me. But I don't really know what perfect love is. I think I have to be happy with what I have."

"I don't think Michael really needs me," Rosie said. "He wants me, sometimes."

"Isn't that lust?"

"Maybe I think love is selflessness," Rosie said. "Michael seems selfless sometimes. But he's too busy."

"He's good at his profession. He's probably selfless to everyone but the ones close to him," Catherine said.

"Love is feeling," Rosie said. "There must be doctors somewhere who can work and feel at the same time. But they're hard to find."

"Maybe Michael is one of those," Catherine said. "It might just take time."

"Clayton is not?"

Catherine smiled. "Definitely not. He thinks of me more like a figurine of Boehm porcelain than as an eternal companion. It's maddening."

Rosie thought for a moment. "I don't think Michael yearns for me."

"I don't think Clayton ever yearned for me. He thinks wives need to have perfect manners and defecate behind closed doors."

Rosie smiled, even though she heard pain in Catherine's voice. "I love Michael in so many ways. There's an intensity to it, and a fear that it won't last."

She felt Catherine's hand on hers.

"It's not you . . . or me. I don't think we'll ever know men," Catherine said.

"That doesn't allow me to ignore them," Rosie said.

"It's their apathy toward us that hurts. I'm angry about it most of the time," Catherine said. "Angry because I have to put up with it. I'm trapped. Time goes by. I don't think I'll ever really know true love."

Rosie smiled wistfully. She felt Catherine's strong presence. "Oh, I hope you do. We all deserve it."

She was as sad as Catherine now. Catherine stood up and waited for her.

"You're a good person, Rosie. Michael doesn't deserve you."

"I'm not sure I could ever believe that," Rosie said.

They joined the tour in the gardens for a brief reception where petits fours and demitasses of deep-black, aromatic coffee were served.

That same afternoon, in a hotel conference room, Mike, as chairman of the operating room committee, led the breakout planning session for the OR. The hospital CEO announced that the new wing on the nineteenth floor had been opened for private patients to get VIP care. Clayton announced a marketing program for a new wing for the obese.

At five o'clock Mike made reservations for two at the most elegant restaurant of the five in the complex. He called Rosie and told her to be ready at seven. He wanted to please her.

He went to the dean's reception on the lawn under one of the live oaks to make the expected contacts, mostly junior faculty needing referrals or committee appointments, and then left to meet Rosemary at the reflecting pond in front of the main house.

Rosie had dressed in white pants and a lavender blouse, accenting her look with a red belt and shoes, and a white and yellow polka-dotted scarf. She asked what he thought.

She was striking. She had sharp features, interestingly arranged. She was an artist. She did big canvases with larger-than-life figures, and oversize sculptures cast in bronze. She was fit from climbing ladders and heavy lifting.

"No one can do it like you," he said.

"Too artsy?"

"This crowd needs artsy. Needs you," he said.

Their table for two was outside and secluded, near the railing of the second-floor gallery that surrounded the house. They looked out onto the expanse of the grounds, vibrant with smoldering streaks of light from the sunset piercing through the live oaks' dark green foliage. They ordered drinks and he asked about her day, and the antiques lecture-tour to three plantation houses.

"I spent some time on the tour with Catherine Otherson."

He couldn't imagine elegant Catherine getting on and off a tour bus full of faculty wives and significant others.

"She talked to me," Rosie said. "A lot. We sat next to each other."

The waiter brought the drinks.

"She doesn't seem happy with marriage," she continued. "I think her marriage really sucks."

"She said that?"

"Not directly. But she had a sadness about her. It came over her like a dark cloud. And then she talked. About her husband, her daughter. She asked about you and me."

Mike ordered dinner for them both and another round of wine.

"Catherine wanted to know how I felt about you," she said, looking at him directly.

He took a sip of his wine. She looked down. As the silence extended, he waved to the waiter and asked him to open the bottle of white wine.

"What did you say?" he asked.

She gave a strained laugh he couldn't interpret. "I asked her how she felt about Clayton."

He touched the top of her hand and smiled.

"Clever," he said.

She smiled.

"Did you have a good time?" he asked.

"I think we both came back feeling ignored by surgeons."

He looked down for a few seconds, then he looked at her.

"That's strange. You don't feel right about you and me?"

"It's not that. It's complicated. I wish we had more time together."

He sipped his wine. "We can do it," he said. "If that's what you want. I just have to schedule better."

The bisque came in bowls hidden under silver-plated domes.

"I felt small around Catherine," she said.

"She talk down to you?"

"Oh, no. Nothing like that. She's so successful. In a different class."

"She could never create what you've created," he said. "You've created beauty. She'd never be able to do that."

"She makes a difference, Michael. She is somebody."

"You're too hard on yourself."

Rosie took a long sip of wine. "Maybe," she said.

The final meetings on Sunday lasted all day, but Michael decided to leave early. Rosie waited in the room until the morning sessions were finished. Michael returned at noon, and in a few minutes they were in the sedan headed for New Orleans – back down the river road, across the bridge to the east bank, then on the I-10 past the airport and into the city.

He talked about the meeting and the weekend, but she didn't say much, unable to shed her anxieties and converse. When they reached the inner city, she turned down the radio.

"I'm concerned about us, Michael. I've been thinking." She looked out the side window. "I don't feel right going on."

He thought for a few seconds. "Don't be ridiculous," he said. "We're right for each other."

He exited the expressway overpass near the Superdome.

"You're special," he said.

"You make me feel special sometimes. I've cherished that."

He glanced at her briefly. "Well, you are."

She was still looking out the window. "But I can't believe it anymore. What you can give is not enough."

"Was it taking to Catherine? Is that what this is about?"

"I was thinking about it before then."

"But it was what she said? About us?"

"No. She just said surgeons were different."

"Than what?"

"I don't know."

"Than women?"

"Yes. That's part of it. But they don't have time for others. They live their work."

She breathed deeply. She was locked-in serious about this.

"I can change, Rosie. Just tell me what to do," he said.

He turned onto Claiborne heading for her shotgun apartment. She stared straight ahead.

"Don't be complicated," he said, smiling to her. "You mean a lot to me."

She felt trapped between fear of a future together and fear of a future not together. She couldn't respond.

"I love you," he said. "I mean it."

She stayed silent. It was actually one of the rare times he had ever said "I love you" without sex involved. But even now it was an echo, slightly hollow. Not insincere. He was too honest to lie. He just didn't know what love meant to her. She knew she would never be the one to allow him to discover what a woman needed. And she knew if they went on he might very well find the one to love, leave her, and she would never recover.

"You've always known I love you," he said. "What's changed?"

She opened her door.

"Let's be close again," he said.

Her face had tensed into an expressionless mask. "Please open the trunk," she said.

He took her bags out of the trunk. She tried to take them out of his hands. "I can manage," she said.

"I can carry your bags, Rosie."

But she took them away from him. He followed her up the porch steps to her door.

"Thanks for everything," she said. "I had a great time."

"Hey. Let's talk at my place for a while," he said. "We can work this out."

"I don't think so." She unlocked the front door. "I need time to recalibrate."

She took her bags and went in. He started to follow.

"I want to be alone," she said, not able to face him.

"Please don't do this," he said.

She closed the door.

She stood motionless inside the door for many seconds. He knocked and waited. She loved him. She loved him too much to let it go on. All he had to do was convince her he cared. But he couldn't do that. He didn't care enough.

He called her the next day and she answered pleasantly but had no time to talk. He called back later but she didn't pick up. He left messages; she would not respond.

She did see him a few more times, unplanned times with stiff greetings between them, and she spoke in impersonal tones and asked disinterested questions. Eventually he seemed to know she would not risk her future with him, and his calling became less frequent. She wasn't surprised when she felt relief.

⚜ PART TWO ⚜

CHAPTER 6

Helen Rappaport was sixteen; she'd missed the birthday party her mother had planned last week – or was it two weeks ago? She hadn't been home. She'd been sleeping in the park or near the river.

In the hours after midnight, the lights dimmed and a deep-space silence enveloped the sounds of street traffic and a rare trolley car. Tourists on Decatur Street were busy finding another party, their blunt shouts and sharp curses piercing the humid air like a knife through lard. But they were too far away for her to attract their attention. Her moment of hope faded.

She leaned against a concrete barrier near the streetcar tracks, her feet out; she eased the pains in her chest and legs with soft moans. Blood oozed from her nose, and a darkening bruise on the side of her face was beginning to ache and throb. She could feel it swelling.

A shadow moved near the streetlamp across the streetcar tracks near the levee and she thought the black angel had come for her. A halo of dreadlocks. She was not afraid. She could welcome death even though she knew she would be in hell. But she was in hell here on earth, so what the hey. The angel left, on foot. She had wanted him to fly, to hover above the trees on the pewter swath of the near-full moon.

She lost the sense of time passing. A woman cop locked the doors in the black and white cruiser, and she curled up on the back seat. Her stomach was big and hurting. Light from the dashboard filtered into the back through the tight mesh screen, leaving diamond-shaped patches on the back of the seat.

On a gurney, the intense light of the emergency room made her eyes squeeze shut. She tried to remember the name of the doctor who was her father's friend. God, if she could only remember. She'd been damn near killed by the trainees at this butchery more than once. Goddamn it. What was his name?

Mike was on in-house trauma faculty-backup call. As was protocol, house staff saw Helen first, and although she was only half conscious, Mike Boudreaux's name floated out from Helen's jumble of misconnected words. Her father knew Dr. Boudreaux, she'd said twice.

That this wretched kid knew a prominent surgeon on staff impressed the fellow, Rich, and he called the on-call room directly.

"She's from the restaurant family. I don't feel good about this one, Dr. Boudreaux," Rich said. "She's a hooker, got beat up by a pimp or a john."

In minutes Mike joined Rich in the OR scrub room. They prepped side by side over a sink and monitored the OR preparations through a rectangular window.

"You know her well?" Rich asked.

"Seen her a few times. I krewed with her father on Bacchus," he said.

Staff positioned the girl on the table as they scrubbed. Her belly was distended from internal bleeding. Her nose was crushed, her left eye swollen, the side of her face purple, and her left arm splinted until the fracture could be reduced when she was out of danger. Anesthesia was having trouble keeping her blood pressure up.

Mike assisted as Rich cut a clean first incision; they were in the abdomen in a minute. Blood gushed. With suction and sponges they cleared the field to see the anatomy.

"One ten over sixty-five," the anesthetist said from behind her barrier drape.

In two minutes Rich had isolated the ruptured spleen, controlling the bleeding – tamponading with sponges and tying off ruptured vessels.

"I'm giving her another unit," the anesthetist said.

They worked with controlled immediacy. Forty-five minutes later, they placed the last staple in closure.

Mike went with Rich to the family waiting room. Helen's father,

Marcel Rappaport, leaned against the small waiting room wall, his arms outstretched, his palms flat on the beige painted surface. His face was flushed. He was alone.

"Jesus, Boudreaux. It took you long enough," Rappaport said.

"She's going to be okay," Mike said, uncomfortable with Marcel's belligerence.

Rappaport shrugged.

"She was assaulted," he added.

"She's a whore, Boudreaux. A drug addict. One screwed-up kid." Marcel Rappaport kept his eyes diverted. "I haven't seen her for months. She lives with her mother when she's not on the streets. That bitch of a wife has a restraining order on me."

"Helen will be out of recovery in a couple of hours." She would survive these wounds, although he was not sure she could survive this life much longer.

"I'm not going to wait around." Rappaport threw his hands up in the air.

"Why show up?" Mike asked. He never remembered Marcel being so exasperating.

"Some nut in the admissions office told me she might die. I got in the car like some diseased homing pigeon. I expected to bury her. Then I got to thinking. Sometimes I think it would be a relief. But she'll live. And we don't get along. And I don't want to relive what we've gone through every time we've talked over the last few years."

"She'll need you," Mike said.

"She's had too many chances, Boudreaux. I'm telling you. I'm not doing anything more."

"Could you give me your cell in case there are complications?" Rich said.

"Pester her mother."

Rappaport yanked the door open.

"She'll need rehab," Mike said.

"She needs a brain transplant," Rapport said without looking back.

"Great guy," Rich said. "Word gets out, everyone will want him for a father."

They walked down the hall toward the doctors' dressing room.

"It's sad," Rich said. "Cases like this. We save her life and her parents don't care. *She* doesn't even care."

"Call Angie Picard," Mike said. "She's the best with these cases. Maybe she can help."

Helen improved. Her temperature was normal, vital signs stable, and she required less pain medication.

Five days after her surgery, Mike directed Angie Picard, a social worker, to a seat in his office. She was effective and well liked.

He came around from behind his desk to an armchair near her. She smiled sincerely, conveying quick intelligence.

"It's Helen Rappaport's father," she said. "He won't talk to me. I've called, written hand-delivered letters. I want good rehab for Helen. He's a basket case, Angie."

"And a negligent father."

"He wasn't always like this. I knew him when he carried pictures of his family in his wallet and passed them around without being asked. He loved Helen."

Angie fingered the edge of Helen's folder.

"She's failed in every program in the city," Angie said. "I want to get her to upscale rehab in Mobile."

"The mother has beaucoup cash from the divorce."

"I'm not sure. She says she's broke. And she hangs up at the sound of Helen's name. You know Rappaport. Maybe you could convince him to support Helen. He wouldn't turn you down, would he?"

"He's moody," Mike said. "Unpredictable." He looked at the concern in Angie's face. How could anyone do her job? She was an accomplished, talented woman with two degrees more than anyone else in her field. She was from a generations-old New Orleans family with a swamp load of money; she could live a life of luxury, but she was passionate about her work. He could not turn her down.

"I'll try," he said. "Tonight."

He pulled into the parking lot of Rappaport's Cajun restaurant, serving seafood and steaks. At ten o'clock the lights went off on the rectangular sign jutting two stories above the street. He waited until

Marcel exited the side door of the building, and then walked up to him.

"Could we talk about Helen, Marcel?"

"Jesus, Boudreaux. I'm wiped out. I've told you I don't want to talk." Mike matched Marcel's tired steps. "What's in it for you?"

"Angie Picard asked me. The social worker. She takes good care of my patients."

They walked to Marcel's burgundy Mercedes sedan. Marcel punched his remote and the locks opened.

"Five minutes," Marcel said. "Get in."

Mike settled into the comfortable leather seat. Marcel took a pint of Russian vodka out of the glove compartment; an automatic pistol gleamed in the dim light. Mike stared.

"Got a permit. Been robbed four times in three months," Marcel said.

"In your car?"

Marcel nodded. "Twice. Shot a carjacker in February on Lakeshore. I wish I'd killed the sonofabitch. Now he's suing me."

Marcel took a healthy swig from the bottle and passed it. Mike declined.

"I came about Helen," Mike said.

"I haven't seen Helen since the divorce," Marcel said. "I can't help. I told you. Her mother has custody. The restraining order is still in effect as far as I know."

"Helen needs rehab. Angie Picard needs you to cover the costs. You don't want her buried in social services."

"I got no insurance. You don't have a clue what went down, Boudreaux. All expensive shit. There is no way!"

"You can't deny Helen a chance to pull her life together. Angie has faith in her."

"Goddamn it, Boudreaux. Helen's hopeless. I've put her in rehab three times already."

Marcel took another swig. He still had half a pint left. His voice was softer, his diction already slurred. "I'm fucking tired of trying to make things right for her."

Marcel slipped into a silence. Mike stared ahead at the dark shadows of a live oak on the lawn nearby. This was a waste of time.

"I gotta tell you, Boudreaux," Marcel began, "she wasn't always a bad kid. But about ten or eleven, she got weird. Blowing off schoolwork. Kept to herself in her room. Slipped out at night. That sort of shit.

"I thought it was teenager time. But she was being fucked over by some adult. I go to the guy, who laughs at me and I tell him I'm going straight to the cops. Sink his ass forever.

"Within an hour, the guy's father, one rich motherfucker, comes to me and my wife. He says the charges would never stick, that he had that kind of power. Did we really want to smear Helen over New Orleans as a victim of sex? Then he says she enjoyed it, and it was her hormones that attracted a man anyway."

Marcel paused. A breeze had picked up, and the faint light shimmered on the oak leaves. "He let me know if I went further, spread the word, he'd blow up the business with my family in it. Believe me, he wasn't just sucking wind."

Mike said nothing.

Marcel found his bottle again and took a slow sip. "It got worse. The sonofabitch puts an envelope with five hundred thousand dollars on my desk. Right here in this restaurant. And we took it. Jesus Christ. We took the money."

Mike looked out the side window at the two empty parking spaces, then to Marcel.

Marcel had a spot of wetness in the stubble of his beard. "Well, it broke up our shitty marriage. I blamed the wife for weakness. She said I sold our daughter. Helen turned into the toughest broad, like some fucking dyke. She does sex for drug money. She hates men. She'll never marry. And she won't talk to me." Marcel wiped away the few more tears. "Is that what you wanted to hear?" he asked.

"Of course not."

"I think about killing myself. If I had any guts, it's what I'd do. I live with a coward in me, or I'd just take that thing . . ." he nodded toward the glove compartment, ". . . and do it. I swear."

The car windows were up. Mike sweated.

Marcel sighed. "Go home, Boudreaux," he finally said. "Relax. I'll try to work it out. I don't like it but I'll do what I can."

Once outside the car, Mike leaned over before closing the door. "You okay to drive?" he asked.

"It would be a blessing," Marcel said.

Mike closed the door gently. Marcel turned over the engine and backed away with the skill of a race driver. He had had years of experience driving while zonked; a slow death from chronic alcohol consumption would kill him before a car crash.

Marcel stopped on his way out of the lot and lowered his window. "I care about Helen," he said to Mike. "You think I don't, but I do." The window slid up smoothly.

CHAPTER 7

Helen was discharged from the hospital. Her belly had sharp pains when she moved. Her left eye was still swollen shut. But it was her arm that gave her a deep, boring pain that kept her from sleeping and on the edge of exhaustion so she could barely think. Angie Picard drove her to a halfway house. In her narrow, sparsely furnished room, she lay on a single bed on her side with her arm propped up on two pillows and took painkillers whenever the staff allowed. She had no appetite.

Three days later Angie Picard came and drove her to Mobile. Her father had helped. He had some motive she didn't know. You couldn't trust the son of a bitch. Her nausea got worse with car motion and she counted the minutes until they arrived. The idea that she might never return to New Orleans came to her through her pain as Angie said goodbye and wished her good luck. With grave seriousness, Angie said that this was the best clinic on the Gulf, and a chance to turn her life around.

In the silence after Angie left, she wondered what it would be like if she never went back to New Orleans. Was that why she was here? She had no home, really. No family any more. The idea of not going home didn't make her sad, but it didn't make her happy, either. It was the way she'd been thinking as long as she could remember. Thinking about how to dull her fears about everything, but she could find nothing she could reach out and grasp – or even describe – that would help. Booze and crack mostly dulled the fear for a few hours, so she could forget. Her craving was not drinking or smoking, but just not having to think about being afraid of something she couldn't name and that could, in the next moment of her life, make her feel so bad.

The pains never left over the next few months as she recovered. But she did find a friend from Atlanta, Jeannena, who liked the music she liked. Together they dreamed a little. They told stories, laughing at themselves. Helen remembered stories that surprised her, stories that were unbelievably similar to Jeannena's when they shared them. Helen found it easy to describe them, because they seemed remote and not really hers.

Over many weeks, she felt a sliver of satisfaction. It was hope, really, that she wouldn't fall into the slide that would carry her down, angry and fighting, to dump her out in the back of a police car on the way to have doctors probe and cut her so she could lie in pain begging a nurse's aide for some hit to ease her. She saw a possible fear-free future, craving nothing but a good night's sleep and tasty fresh fruit for breakfast. She found looking forward to moments of dreadless calm strangely intoxicating. She wanted never to lose it.

Her image in the mirror changed from day to day. In those thoughtless days of passing out for a few hours' rest, on gravel or grass as the softest surface she could find, she never saw herself in a mirror, and would never have looked, even in a restroom mirror or a reflective store window. She had no wish to see herself in those days. As she healed, she first looked at her face. The bruises had faded, the scabs dropped off. And then, gradually, she began going to the bathroom daily to deliberately look at the face staring back, searching for changes. She combed her hair. Put on a little makeup. Wore only a freshly washed T-shirt and jeans at first, but then later a print dress.

She felt joy when Jeannena said one day, "Hey, girl, you something when you get it together. Like, it swings, baby." You too, Helen replied.

Helen had begun to enjoy emotions, one at a time, one after the other. But when her mother showed up unannounced, she felt the return of a spaghetti tangle of interest, suspicion, pride, distrust, guilt, uncertainty, doubt, inaction . . . and the fear . . . like a shark fin in muddy water. She and her mother sat speechless for her half-hour visit, but then her mother announced she would pick her up in two weeks to take her home. Mother had a new boyfriend, a drummer, who lived in the house with her now, and he had agreed to let Helen live with them until she could get out on her own.

Do I really want to go back to New Orleans? she thought. She wasn't sure. As the reality settled in, she had fear, no joy.

"You've put on weight," her mother said before they had crossed the Alabama line on the way home. Helen ignored her, the way she had in the years before her mother had disowned her. "You were always so pretty."

It was dark as they drove through Biloxi, Gulfport, Pass Christian. Casino billboard lights animated gyrating figures of girls and fish and horses.

"Don't be so sullen," her mother said as they crossed the Louisiana state line.

Helen turned her head away with her eyes tightly shut.

CHAPTER 8

When Mike arrived for the task force meeting, the only one waiting was the assistant dean who would chair the meeting. The dean handed him the mission statement: "To evaluate the present status of bariatric surgery for the obese."

"That's not what we're about," Mike said. "'To evaluate.' We need to set indications."

"I don't want this job. And I don't want your advice," the dean said.

Thirty minutes later, Hammond McLaughlin, as chairman of the department of surgery, welcomed and introduced each member, beginning with the non-surgeons – a psychiatrist, an internist, a pediatrician, an assistant to the hospital CEO, the dean for clinical affairs, a research coordinator, and the department administrator – then listed the surgeons. Of the four general surgeons, all had done bariatric surgery on the obese as a procedure, but only Clayton had developed it as a major part of elective general surgery.

McLaughlin called Clayton to the podium to update the non-surgeons on what the service was doing. Clayton spoke without notes. He feigned modesty. The morbidly obese who could not control their weight with diet, drugs, and therapy, he said, could be surgically treated with one of two procedures at the center. He explained details of lap band surgery, which restricted the volume of the stomach, and gastric bypass surgery, the Roux-en-Y procedure that reconnects parts of the digestive tract to bypass most of the stomach and prevent absorption. Procedures could be done through a small tube, the laparoscope, or through an open – and much wider – incision in the abdominal wall. Laparoscopic surgery was more difficult and had a higher complication rate than open-incision surgery, especially during the difficult early learning period for surgeons. Clayton proudly announced that ninety percent of the service's obese cases were laparoscopic now, and that both mortality and morbidity rates were acceptable. Then chairman McLaughlin called on Mike to present the surgical coordinator's data.

Mike stated facts and aimed no criticism at individual surgeons. He compared their obese service to that of other institutions. He concluded, "It is true we need a comprehensive program to treat these patients, but we must determine the right patient for the right procedure, and operate only when needed so we can reasonably predict results."

A mixed silence of sympathy, hostility, and apathy hung in the room. Mike waited for questions.

Slowly Clayton rose from the back row. His voice carried over the group, with an accent of rolled vowels and soft consonants that seemed more intense than usual.

"I know what it is to be fat. Patient after patient tells me of the taunts, how they fought through the derision. And I tell you, Boudreaux, there is nothing we can do for patients that is more important than this surgery. You don't do the surgery enough to comment. Besides, you're not fat. And what you present is unreasonable and restrictive to patients who need the surgery." Clayton sat down.

The assistant dean led the discussion. "We can't restrict licensed surgeons with established privileges from doing their work," was the prevalent comment.

"Maybe a voluntary monitoring system," one suggested.

"Legal ramifications from restrictions could be costly and time consuming," an administrator noted.

"We need standards."

"Sanctions."

"A moratorium until we've got it sorted out."

"Any action must be approved by the faculty senate."

"This is not an academic issue. This is clinical. We need a change in hospital bylaws."

But after two hours of discussion, no indications were clarified, no changes in existing indications proposed. The task force refused to make a commitment to nonsurgical treatment, fearing that public exposure of the information would dampen referrals.

Committees were assigned to investigate, study, and present alternative guidelines. It was obstructive delay. Many in the room thought that if they ignored things long enough, the problem would resolve itself.

The meeting was adjourned. It would take weeks, maybe months, to get definitive action, even if a decision for action finally could be agreed upon.

Clayton continued to operate. Mike and other faculty monitored him from a distance. In two months, Clayton's volume of obese cases almost doubled, but he made no technical errors that threatened a patient. At first Clayton did not do laparoscopy, and relied as required on the open-incision technique. But recently he'd gone back to laparoscopy, and he hadn't finished his training, in defiance of his agreement with the department. Clayton refused to discuss it with Mike or the chair, nor would he present a proof of completion of training report.

CHAPTER 9

Breezeless late-summer air descended on New Orleans like a hot, transparent fog as the fifth hurricane of the season, Deon, intensified in the Gulf to a category three.

For Mike, tracking hurricanes on radio or TV was time consuming and mostly useless. He relied on word of mouth and reacted only when the threat was imminent. But at five o'clock in the morning on the day of predicted landfall, the caretaker for his house in the Quarter began boarding up windows and filling bathtubs and sinks with water. He planned for three days at the hospital, packing a suitcase with clothing changes and bathroom essentials.

By midafternoon the hospital staff began discharging elective and noncritical patients, prepared for power outages, as remaining critical patients would depend on emergency generators, and called in off-duty personnel. At four o'clock he went to check on his mother. She was seventy-five now, and he always stopped by to help her board up before storms.

He loved his mother. She lived above her shop near the park on Magazine Street where she sold remedies and herbs, aromas and essences, mojos and spell kits, and gave advice to customers, most of whom were friends. She had never married. His father had left her before he was born, and her Cajun-Catholic family had disowned her for a few decades. He loved her for all her eccentricities. He was proud of how she had supported herself as a medium and fortune-teller in and around Jackson Square since the sixties. She was a regular stop for tourists, and a friend and confessor to any native who needed her, usually without charge. But in recent times, the people of Jackson Square had switched from good wines to bad drugs, kind words to violent curses, and she had decided to move uptown to sell her merchandise.

She had a hammer and nails on the kitchen table. She scolded him. He had not been by often enough. He retrieved planks from under the house to board up the windows. He wired the upstairs shutters closed, and taped up vulnerable panes of glass.

As he worked, Mother Boudreaux drew water from the tap and filled bottles and pans. "You see Rosemary, Michael? She say you not by her for *longtemps*."

"I've been operating day and night the past month."

"You've found someone else!"

"No one, mom."

She switched bottles under the water flow. She glared at him. The silence grew.

"You marry that Rosie, Michael. Last time she here, she find a new beaux, you know. She say that to your mother."

"She's a divorced Catholic, mother. I can't imagine her getting married again." But the news disturbed him.

"She don't love no one else. She love you."

Mother capped the water bottles. She'd mellowed her conceit on divorce. She was a romantic.

He checked her food and medicine supply; she had stocked well.

His mother turned silent.

"I'll call from the hospital to check on you," he said.

"You think about that woman more, n'est-ce pas?"

"As soon as I can after the storm, mom."

"It is not good, this letting the good horse out of the barn to roam the pastures." She wanted grandchildren, and she blamed him for not providing them. All her friends had grandchildren.

He kissed his mother on the cheek as he left. He would worry about her during the storm. He did not insist that she stay with friends or hire someone to help her prepare. He'd tried that before, and she'd been insulted. Her independence kept her going, and she didn't like suggestions that she wasn't competent.

He drove back toward the hospital along Tchoupitoulas Street. The winds blew harder, bending saplings, whipping leaves and papers into the air. He went north on Poydras toward Tulane. As he neared the multi-decked garage for patients and employees, he saw Angie Picard standing in the rain next to her car with no rain gear on. She was trying to push a three-thousand-pound vehicle to the side of the street. He stopped and got out, shielding his eyes from the water.

"You steer, I'll push," he said.

Once her car was curbside, Angie got into Mike's car. He drove toward the security office to let her off.

"Do you remember Helen Rappaport?" Angie asked.

"I've thought about her often," he said.

"She's gained confidence. Back living with her mother. Even looking for a job. Her recovery was beyond expectations."

"I hope Marcel's happy."

"She says she sees him twice a week."

He knew Angie's care had been responsible for Helen's successful reentry into the functional world. He could imagine how thankful Marcel must be, but knew he was not the type to allow gratitude to slip out through his hard-baked exterior.

The hurricane made landfall west of New Orleans; the damage was mild and the cleanup not too onerous. The hospital received few casualties, and the people of New Orleans prayed in thanks that the big one they dreaded had not chosen them this time.

When he was off call on Sunday two weeks later, he went to Mass at St. Louis Cathedral. He arrived late and found space in the center near the rear. He searched the congregation. Rosie usually worshiped in front to the right. The sermon was long and heavy on the spiritual value of fasting. He thought he'd missed her until she rose to leave; she was alone. He'd half expected to see a male companion.

He caught up to her and walked alongside.

"Hey. It's me. Mike," he said. "Not dangerous. Feeling friendly. And willing to buy a beautiful woman a cup of coffee."

"You're hopeless," she said. She did not smile.

"But likeable."

"Really, Michael."

"You've disappeared. Mother said you'd been by."

"You're the one who disappeared."

"A new boyfriend?"

She looked at him. "A coffee. That's all."

"That's what mother said. You had a new beaux."

"I have a new interest. I do."

"We can sit on a bench in the alley," he said. Notes from a calliope on the paddle-wheel river steamer danced through the streets. Tourists clumped together on street corners and at store windows. There was the smell of coffee, and takeout food, and pot lingering from the night before.

He bought coffees and they sat together on a backless stone bench in front of a block-stone wall near Decatur Street. She kept two feet of space between them.

"Do you love this guy?" he asked.

"He loves to cook. He's a sous chef. I've known him for years."

She looked off across the street. A jazz band was setting up under a tent for the Sunday brunch crowd at a restaurant with outdoor covered seating. He missed her. He wanted her back like they'd been.

"You getting married?" he asked.

"He doesn't know it yet, but yes."

"You won't change your mind?"

They sat in silence for minutes.

"I'm happy, Michael." She stood. He stayed seated. "I am really happy."

"Without me? You said you'd never get married again."

"I changed."

He didn't want her happy without him. He missed her. Damn it. He was jealous.

"Is there something I can do to work it out?" Would she move in with him?

"It's not you," she said. "It's me. I just need more than you can give." She stared at him dry-eyed. "It strings me out."

He was irritated now. It was unreasonable. They had always spent their free time together. But he would not plead. If she had found someone better, okay. He wasn't going to grovel. He'd given her his best. If it wasn't good enough, so be it.

She drained her cup. "It was great, but it's time to move on," she said.

She hesitated but didn't continue. Would she say more? Say she was sorry? That she couldn't do without him and she was going against what she really wanted?

But she walked away.

What did that silence mean? Had he really meant so little to her? She *was* important to him. He needed to talk more.

"Take care," he finally said in a not-too-loud voice.

Had she heard? Did she look back? . . . No, probably not.

He didn't move for many minutes. He was oppressed by a sense of finality. He wondered about what he had lost. He wondered, too, if he'd ever have a chance to revive it. She couldn't really be serious about a sous chef, could she?

CHAPTER 10

Mike was surprised when Helen Rappaport entered his office with her mother, Pamela. He hadn't seen Pamela for years. She'd changed a lot. She had the foundations of an attractive woman, but her flesh sagged now, and the lines on her face had taken on permanent slants of smoldering anger and disappointment. Helen was her only child.

Helen smiled widely. Dental work had filled spaces from lost teeth. Her clean hair was trimmed and framed a healed, healthy face. He looked at her record. Drug free for months. But she had gained weight. A lot.

"I've placed her on diets," Pamela explained to Mike after brief greetings, "but she has no willpower."

Clayton Otherson had finished Helen's examination two days ago, and the nurse had put her lab and imaging results in her medical record folder.

"Dr. Otherson recommends the surgery," Pamela said, her teeth clenched. "But Marcel wants you. That's why we came."

Helen fidgeted.

"I'd like to talk to Helen for a few minutes," he said.

"I have the right to be here," Pamela said.

"And you will be. Please. Just for a few minutes."

Pamela left the room, closing the door firmly.

Helen looked at nothing on the floor.

"What do *you* want, Helen?"

Helen clasped her hands in her lap. She looked away from him.

"I know what you've been through. You've done well."

"I gained weight."

"But you're not obese."

"Tell that to my mother." Helen looked up, but her eyes avoided him. "I've already had liposuction."

"Many doctors would think you're too young for the surgery."

Helen slumped as if she'd finished with responses.

"I can't recommend surgery," he said. "I don't think you're a candidate. But I want to know how you feel."

Helen seemed to sigh, but there was no sound or movement.

"I don't want to argue about it anymore," she said. Her eyes were vacant; she searched for a comfortable spot to look after looking at him for an instant.

"I'm going to recommend a dietitian who works with young people. Would that be okay?"

Helen shrugged.

"I need your approval."

"Whatever."

He went to the door and asked Pamela to return. He recommended diet and exercise, and counseling to develop good lifestyle changes.

"She won't diet. I told you. She has no discipline." Pamela's speech turned sharp. "Dr. Otherson says the surgery can do good. He's the expert. We came here only because Marcel knows you."

That was awkward. Dr. Otherson was promoted as the expert, but he wasn't the best surgeon available. Still, to be ethical, you never talked down the skill of a practicing surgeon. Surgery was almost always a judgment based on partial information, not fact, and unjust criticism was unfairly hurtful. So you had to keep quiet. And you expected others to do the same for you. "I don't do many bariatric cases," Mike said. "Still, I recommend another try at weight control based on the knowledge in the literature about the procedure."

"She's impossible," Pamela said. "She's negative. Negative about everything. And the way she looks!"

He watched Helen carefully for a reaction, but she'd run out of will to make decisions or disagree.

"I can arrange an appointment with a specialist," Mike said.

"A surgeon?"

"No."

"I don't want more consultations with do-nothings," Pamela said.

He looked to Helen. "What would you like?"

Helen shrugged.

Pamela stood and grabbed Helen's arm and pulled her into a standing position.

"This has not been helpful," she said over her shoulder as they left the room.

He noted his recommendations in the chart and dictated a detailed letter to Clayton. He called on the intercom for the next patient consultation.

CHAPTER 11

Two weeks later, Mike received an invitation from Catherine and Clayton Otherson for a beach party celebration for the new member of the department, the recipient of the surgical award Catherine had successfully raised funds for. It was a departmental event, in a way, one of the invitations Mike felt he could not turn down as chief of service.

He arrived at Grand Isle just before midnight. Moderate cloud cover blanketed the moonlight, and the sea was tar black under a dark sky. No space was left between the eight vehicles lined side by side in the two drives, and he parked on the street. The Otherson house was dark. On the screen door, safety pinned to the screen at eye level, was a welcome note, handwritten and addressed to Dr. Boudreaux, with directions to what was to be his bedroom in the Blantons' house next door (they were out of the country, the note said).

The Blantons' front door was unlocked. He heard sleeping sounds from a back master bedroom and left the interior lights off. He found his bedroom, stripped to his underwear, brushed his teeth, and slipped under the covers of the double bed. Surf sounds pulsed into the room through an open window, and a gentle offshore breeze rustled the white sheers that framed the half-open window shade. It flapped briefly in the occasional gust. The smell of the ocean carried the musk of seaweed and a faint stench of dying and dead shellfish.

He slept fitfully. At dawn, a toilet flushed, followed by silence except for the surf and the cries of gulls. He waited until the sun was well above the horizon before dressing in rumpled chinos and a T-shirt, and walking over to the Otherson beach house. The sparse grass was bent with dew and glinted in the sun. To the southwest, clouds blocked out the sky over the Gulf. A front had stalled. He entered the house through the back door, lugging food and drink he had brought from New Orleans.

Catherine was in the kitchen. "Did you see Alice and Peter?" she said.

"I heard them."

"She's sick with her pregnancy." She made no effort to look at him.

Catherine wore shorts and a man's button-down light-blue dress shirt, frayed at the collar, and was toasting English muffins and pan-frying bacon strips. He placed pastries and wine bottles on the counter and stacked beer next to the refrigerator.

Catherine thanked him for his contributions and told him to pour himself coffee. Her daughter Mellissa slouched on the sofa in the family room. None of the guests were out of their bedrooms yet. In the morning light, Mellissa seemed to have more of Catherine's perfect facial symmetry than Clayton's seemingly randomly collected features.

"Say hello to Dr. Boudreaux," Catherine said to Mellissa.

Mellissa had on flip-flops and a two-piece bathing suit that exposed long legs. Her calves and thighs curved beyond the expectations of adolescence, but immature breasts left her halter top with loose folds. She said nothing, intent on a handheld electronic game that was the rage with kids half her age. Catherine handed him muffins and bacon on a small plate. Mellissa pushed away a plate offered to her.

"It's a long time before lunch, Mellissa," Catherine said. "No snacking."

Alice and Peter Ravenel came in. Catherine pointed to the central island where they could choose their breakfast from the food she had laid out.

Mike sat on the sofa two feet from Mellissa; she turned her shoulders away from him and concentrated on her game.

As they ate, Catherine talked to the Ravenels of storms, and waves, and beach erosion. Mike listened. Peter had more pride in his professional accomplishments than Mike thought appropriate for a beginner.

"I thank you and Dr. Otherson," Peter said to Catherine, "for the endowed fellowship."

The winner had not yet been publicly announced. Maybe that was one reason for the party.

"Thank Surgigen," Catherine said.

"Dr. McLaughlin told me of your work with the alumni," Peter said.

Wife Alice said she had majored in social science at Oklahoma. Proud, too, she was, that her choice of a major had prepared her for the world. Now she was proud to be a homemaker and a mother. Mike guessed Peter spent very little time with Alice.

Other party guests were up; doors slammed, toilets flushed in the back. Mike finished eating and took his dishes and utensils to the sink. He approached the passage to the back bedrooms and the kitchen to gaze at the framed photos on the wall. The largest was a regal full-length portrait of Catherine in a strapless white gown as Queen of Rex.

Alice Ravenel stood, her hands protecting her belly, and shuffled over to see what Mike was looking at.

"Those were the days," Catherine called to them.

Three other framed color photos of Catherine in Mardi Gras ball gowns lined the wall: a white satin gown with a full-length cape, a playful lace-trimmed gown with a touch of Midsummer's Night Dream, and a medieval-style ocean-blue gown with a white linen collar.

"I wore that to Orpheus," Catherine said, pointing to the blue from the kitchen. Alice Ravenel silently belched; Mike smelled sour, acid breath. She smiled an insincere apology.

"Amazing," Alice said. But she sounded judgmental, as if she thought it all frivolous. She was new to New Orleans and its ways.

"Clayton decided to marry me after Rex. He was living with his mother. She moved to Baltimore to be with him during training," Catherine said, coming to stand next to Alice.

Peter joined them in front of the pictures.

"Was his father alive?" Alice asked.

"Killed in a deep-sea fishing accident when Clayton was a boy. His mother, Beulah, was a real dowager. She read the same books over and over: *The Moviegoer, Light in August, Lanterns on the Levee, The Awakening.* Clayton warned me, and I read them all twice. That alone convinced her I was worthy of her son."

The Hebert-Otherson wedding was folklore; they were married in the Cathedral with a reception for twelve hundred that included the governors of Louisiana and Texas, two federal judges, three Broadway actors – no movie stars – a painter with collage art in the Whitney, an opera singer with the Met, four CEOs of Fortune 500 companies, and every native New Orleanian with class.

Back in the Blantons' beach house after breakfast, Mike read surgery journals. His mind returned to Catherine's description of her life with Clayton. It wounded vapid and lonely. Alice rested in the back bedroom between frequent trips to the toilet; Peter ran on the beach road to meet his training schedule for a marathon in Washington.

At eleven, Mike put on his swim trunks and a light short-sleeved shirt, and joined everyone next door. Guests with drinks in hand chatted in the crowded family room.

Catherine assigned beach gear she'd organized for everyone to carry, and all the guests, minus Alice and Peter, were off to the beach for a pre-lunch swim. Clayton and Catherine led the way.

The storm front was barely moving. The sky was gray overhead and gave the water a metallic look. The winds were offshore and the Gulf churned rare waves high enough to surf on. Bathers had to bury umbrella poles in the sand as deep as they could to keep them from blowing away.

Clayton set up an umbrella. Mike helped unfold aluminum deck chairs. He walked to the water's edge. He paused to watch as Mellissa first, then Catherine, ran into the water. Catherine wore a tight, one-piece suit designed for least resistance, and Mellissa had a scanty two-piece number, the sparse cloth in the back lost in the crevice between her glutes. Clayton joined him.

"Mellissa's turned into a young lady," Mike said.

"She's too ripe for the boys and too hostile for me," Clayton said. "She thinks Catherine is her captor sometimes. Stays out a lot. Treats her mother with no respect." Clayton loosened his bathing suit string, adjusted the height of the suit and retied. "She's a real pain in the ass sometimes."

"She doing well in school?"

"Not really. You like Peter better now?" Clayton asked.

"Never disliked him, actually. Thought he needed more training."

"His research will bring class to the service. Fat will be called 'obese' from now on."

"There are some pretty deserving clinician scientists in the department," Mike said. "They're working on mechanisms at the basic molecular levels. Prime endowed-chair material."

"We did right, Mike. Peter's got an MPH and an MBA. The clinical stuff is important, too. He'll prove himself," Clayton said.

Others had entered the water and were splashing each other in mock battle. Clayton held up his hand to stop Mike when the water was above their knee level.

"You know, Mike, I didn't appreciate your getting involved in the Rappaport case."

Mike cringed. He obviously hadn't been invited for his personality, or to welcome Peter and Alice.

"She needs that surgery," Clayton continued.

"It was a second opinion, Clayton," he said. "I thought she was too young and not morbidly obese."

"Don't ever talk down a colleague. That's what I taught you."

"I never talked you down."

"That's not what the mother said."

"That woman has serious psychological problems."

Clayton grunted. "You're not acting like one of us, Michael. You're talking like a fucking dermatologist."

Catherine called to them chest-deep in water. "Come on in." She waved.

Mike dove into an oncoming wave, away from Catherine and on an angle to the shore, leaving Clayton thigh deep in water. Once beyond the breakers, he began to swim the crawl straight out into deeper water.

At the Blantons' after his swim, he showered and dressed in shorts and a T-shirt. He crossed again to the Otherson house; guests barely noticed him as they ate sandwiches they'd made themselves.

"Babs and I are taking Mellissa along with Cathy and Harold to play tennis," Catherine said to him. "Do you want to come along?"

Catherine wore tennis white. She had been a tournament player in college.

"I didn't bring tennis stuff," he said.

"Plenty of extra rackets in the closet," she said. "Wear those shorts and your running shoes. We're going to the public courts next to the school." She found a racket. "Try this." She had the experience to guess his grip size; the handle felt large enough.

Catherine called to Mellissa without looking at her. "Are you ready?"

Mellissa still sat on the sofa and didn't respond. She wasn't ready. Two couples were playing scrabble sitting around a folding card table.

"I don't have to play," he said to Catherine, still not enthusiastic.

Catherine ignored him. "Mellissa. Get up." Mellissa stood up. "You'll be Dr. Boudreaux's partner."

Mellissa refused to change clothes; she would play tennis in swimwear and flip-flops. She looked at Mike. "You any good?" she asked.

"Maybe," he said. "Maybe not."

After tennis, Mike saw Alice and Peter Ravenel in the Blanton family room. She sat on a sofa, her face pale, her eyes without sheen, like gauze. She nodded but didn't smile.

"Have a drink," Peter said.

Mike took a Diet Dr. Pepper from the refrigerator. He took a straight-back chair from the kitchen table and sat next to them.

"I'm eager to start the fat surgery," Peter said. "It's a real opportunity."

"Everybody has their own niche," Mike said.

"But you don't do it."

Alice groaned. Peter reached for her. "It'll pass," she said. Peter sat back down.

"You've got a good reputation. Why not do the bariatric stuff?"

Peter asked.

"I don't like the results. Any success with the obese still seems to be a change in lifestyle. And that means messing with the head, not cutting the belly."

"But there are successes."

"Not enough for me. And the weight loss doesn't last as long as it should, for the most part."

"Clayton's got more cases than he can handle," Peter said.

"The public seems ready. The marketing is great. It's just not for me, Peter."

"I think that's a little holier than thou, Mike."

Mike angered at his rudeness. Peter was the new guy. "You think it's so great," he said, "don't charge for the procedure."

Peter clenched his hands together. "That's really unfair."

"You make enough."

"That's bullshit. I got tuitions coming up. Retirement."

"I don't give a damn what you do, Peter. Just don't tell me it's not the money."

Alice heaved and threw up in her hands. Peter jumped up to help. She was wiping her face with the hem of her skirt; her ankles were thick with swelling. Peter helped her to the back bedroom.

Mike put his head back and closed his eyes. At times he thought surgery had made a wrong turn for profit a few years back; and now, with Peter and his quest for fortune, he felt lost in a jungle of ethics and profit.

After dinner, he decided to leave early the next morning. He told Clayton. As he was walking back to the Blantons', Catherine ran up.

"Could you take Mellissa back?"

"At seven AM?"

"She wants to go to church with friends."

He hesitated. "Sure," he said. He shrugged, not thrilled with the idea.

"I'll have her ready and waiting," Catherine said with determination.

In the car the next morning, Mellissa put her feet up on the dashboard. It was the old Lincoln Continental he'd had since med school, immune to damage, but he didn't like her attitude.

"Buckle up," he said.

"I don't like doctors."

"Everybody buckles," he said.

"Not everybody," she said, making no move to find her seatbelt.

He reached across and buckled her in.

She took out a cigarette to light up before they were off the island.

"No smoking," he said.

"You're out of control, man. You're not my father." But she shoved the cigarette back into the pack, breaking it in the middle.

"The beach turn you sour?" Mike asked, and wondered, what was the youngest age to turn into a witch? "And I'm glad I'm not your father."

"What a shitty thing to say," she said.

She moved away from him, straining the seat belt, and looked out the window.

"You play tennis pretty well," he offered.

"You expected me to be worse?"

"I thought you might break an ankle in those flip-flops. But you're a pretty good athlete. Like your mom."

"She played better than you expected, didn't she?"

"I was surprised," he said.

She laughed. "You play young for an old guy."

He concentrated on the driving.

Mellissa reached down into her bag. She pulled up a can of beer and popped the top.

"I suppose you don't allow beer drinking," she said. She swallowed half the contents.

He decided talking to children was not his strong point.

She finished that can and threw it out the open window.

"Don't litter," he said.

She opened a second can. He drove on without comment. This can she drank more slowly, and when she finished, she put the empty can into her bag. She put her head back on the headrest and closed her eyes.

"You like the party?" he asked.

"Mom made me come. Doctors don't exactly rock."

The weather had shifted. Cloud cover gave a gray cast to the countryside, and the world appeared less sharp than in sunlight.

The dashboard clock had stopped working years ago, and he looked at his watch. They should be back by ten fifteen.

Mellissa leaned forward and twisted the radio dial. She swore at the preachers giving sermons, at the country music. She settled for an acid rock sound.

Mike turned the radio down.

"You don't like that," she said.

He ignored her.

"You need a little cool, dude," she said.

"Dr. Boudreaux to you."

She shrugged, leaned back, and closed her eyes. Her mouth opened. She snorted loudly on inhale.

He pulled up to the Otherson mansion forty minutes later and nudged Mellissa with his fist to wake her. She was startled at first, until she discovered she was home. She undid her seat belt.

"I'm *really* glad *you're* not *my* father," she said. She grabbed her bag and got out.

He handed her a key Catherine had given him in case the house staff had not arrived yet and Mellissa had forgotten hers.

CHAPTER 12

Catherine worked alone at the beach house the day after the guests left. Clayton had taken his car to return early in the morning to go to the hospital. As arranged, Mellissa had spent the night with a school friend and would go straight to school from her friend's house.

A caretaker would bring a crew to clean the house later in the week. She worked to secure valuables and pack up the things they could no longer risk leaving in an empty house on the beach. Theft was not epidemic on the island, but it was persistent. Mostly kids and a few professionals had stolen TVs, shotguns, a silver service, cash and credit cards, a kayak, a chainsaw.

The party had not even been a modest success. Probably doomed to failure from the start. She enjoyed entertaining when everything went well; she saw it as a skill, to make people relax and enjoy learning about each other. Of course she couldn't expect too much from the parties where professionals were invited out of obligation. Great parties involved guests carefully chosen, studied for their compatibility. Family weekends generally didn't work well; family dynamics got in the way, and there was universal dread of an explosive confrontation. Dinner parties with independent smart couples were the best. And that's where the surgeons were persistent failures. It was more than the fact that they were all so self-centered. Their worlds were too focused and crammed full of never-ending challenges, bees drawn to their honey-task and driven to return to the hive in a field among vibrant fluttering butterflies and soaring dragonflies with transparent wings and swizzle-stick tails. Most parties needed teamwork. Surgeons failed again on that front. Wives and significant others were more burdens than joys. This weekend was painfully predictable – guarded conversation and snide whispers, for the most part. And all that parting babble about a great time and a wonderful weekend was pure lies – necessary, but still untrue.

Mike Boudreaux had been the only single at the party besides Mellissa. She had worried about him being alone, but he hadn't seemed self-conscious at all. The tennis had animated him. He was surprisingly accomplished and in good shape – he apparently worked out frequently. Even more surprising, he had teased Mellissa into actually trying to improve her game, something she, as a mother, could never do.

She was not sure that placing Mike in the Blanton house with Peter and Alice Ravenel had been a good idea. She was aware of Alice's unhappiness, not only with her pregnancy, which was making her miserable, but she suspected Alice had come to hate Peter in ways that only a marriage could provoke. Had it been an arranged marriage? Certainly not the way she and Clayton had been thrown together for the convenience of social acceptance and advancement. Neither Alice nor Peter had the money or the background for that. And they were from cultures too different to allow arranged marriages for daughters with marginal potential for catching a man. Alice was from the North, Peter from South Carolina. Maybe Alice had latched onto Peter for security. She wasn't pretty. Definitely not sexy. Peter was a good catch for her. In him she likely saw a future of financial stability she had never known. She probably had never known love, either, and had made marriage an intellectual reality for what she thought was best for her and her children.

When they were alone, Alice had mentioned Mike to her. She was attracted to him, Alice hinted. Catherine suspected it was an attraction that Alice had never felt with Peter. Alice had asked questions about Mike. Had he been married? Did Catherine like him? Was he gay? Catherine really didn't know a lot about Mike, who had always been confidently unrevealing on previous social occasions. And most of what she knew, she'd learned from his former girlfriend. The artist, Rosemary. Besides, she would never tell Alice anything personal about Mike, even if she possessed the information. She didn't like Alice. When Alice asked if Mike came to most department parties alone, she had a chance to put the little hussy on another trail.

"He avoids department parties. We rarely see him. He came to the faculty retreat with an artist from the Quarter. A lovely girl, really," she had said matter-of-factly.

"Do they . . . like, live together?" Alice had asked, undeterred by a wave of nausea that made her face pale.

"I don't think so," she answered.

Mike's antennae wouldn't have picked up Alice's vibes. He was too busy for that. And her pregnancy made her more unattractive than she probably had been as a desperate virgin, even if that had been an unlikely virtue.

"He's cute," Alice said in a high voice, as if Mike were a newborn puppy.

Catherine had found herself curious about Mike. Curious, especially about what his true nature was after hearing Rosemary Dayside's unfulfilled longings for him at the faculty retreat. She had not seen any meanness in him during the entire weekend. On the tennis court, he laughed freely, with a sense of humor that was charmingly aimed at himself at times. But he had been guarded, too, and his interest in the other guests was definitely muted. She sensed a capacity for caring, more than most surgeons had. Mike had a caring for humans who were not patients, too. She couldn't exactly pinpoint why she felt that way, but she was sure of it.

After the party, she had fallen asleep wondering about Mike. Clayton breathed heavily in a single bed on the other side of the room. In the pitch dark with her eyes closed, she could see an image of Mike. It was more of a feeling than a picture, but it seemed to exist in front of her somewhere, although never quite real, always starting formless, then with soft-edged details changing one at a time. It never became a complete image. And today, as she packed the silver and the TV sets into the car to take back to the city, the pleasant memory of those pre-sleep images stayed with her, even without the quiet of a dark room after midnight.

CHAPTER 13

The annual fall meeting of the American College of Surgeons was at the convention center in San Francisco. Mike chose carefully which scientific sessions he attended. There were many choices running concurrently. This session was on angiogenesis, presented by a Robinson Award winner. Clayton was not there, and the session was sparsely attended compared to the clinical sessions, which dealt with surgical innovations and techniques.

He liked the science. He liked the exploration of ideas that no one had ever thought of before. If he'd had the time, he would have established a research lab. But that was incompatible with his department's need for clinical productivity. And the school did not support research by MDs hired to be productive.

He chatted with friends during the breaks and ate a bratwurst and drank a soda for lunch from a portable vending cart near the convention center entrance.

At one o'clock, he went to the plenary session. All but a few of the two thousand auditorium seats were taken. Clayton, a member of the board of governors of the college, was giving a talk on bariatric surgery. Clayton had done enough cases to qualify for the accolade "top ten bariatric surgeon in the country." Only large numbers of cases counted for the award; indications for surgery or results were not considered.

Mike moved down the side aisle and leaned against the wall as the current president of the board of regents introduced Clayton, the featured speaker of the day. He noted that Clayton would also be honored this evening at seven o'clock with the presentation of the Penderock Award for distinguished contributions to the advancement of surgery for the obese.

Clayton read his speech. He used only the occasional visual aid, but he presented detailed statistics on what he called the "New Orleans experience." The "experience" presented was generally comparable with what others were experiencing. Nationally, many patients did not lose weight after surgery, and gaining weight after an initial loss was common. Clayton was specific with anecdotal successes, but Mike noted that he did not present detailed quality-of-life data or psychological assessments. Presenting this "soft" data about people's lives would have improved the quality of Clayton's talk.

Clayton finished well. Overall, Mike couldn't suppress a touch of envy at his prominence. Clayton was building a national reputation, and although the procedure definitely wasn't Mike's personal favorite, for those who embraced it, Clayton's reputation was solid and growing outside Louisiana. And he'd made it through the last few months without a major complication.

At the afternoon session, Mike sat next to Clayton in the front row. After the awards presentations, an amazing ob-gyn surgeon from Kenya, famous for her excellent work on girls mutilated with ritual clitorectomy, was to speak.

"Your morning speech was impressive," Mike said.

"Tell that to our OR committee," Clayton replied. "Let them chew on my advancements, and get them off my back."

Mike understood where Clayton was coming from. Janet the orthopedist would not attend this meeting; few orthopedists did, but Mike would make her aware that Clayton was not working in isolation in his surgical treatment of the obese. That was only fair, and if Clayton altered his indications, it might be acceptable to the committee to let him continue, with supervision.

"You ought to do more obese cases, Mike," Clayton said. "You ever think about it?"

"Not yet. I still like the routine stuff and the trauma," Mike said.

The surgeons returned to their seats after the break. On the stage, the meeting coordinators were lining up chairs for the dignitaries and honorees, including Clayton. Clayton's cell phone vibrated. He listened intently. "I'm going to get my award in minutes. Damn it!

Just wait there. I'll be there as soon as I can."

Mike could hear a voice between Clayton's urgent whispers, but he could not make out words. "I've got to go. We're being called to go on stage," Clayton said, and rang off.

Clayton turned to Mike. "Mellissa's been arrested at a protest. She called Catherine from outside a paddy wagon." He paused. "Would you go, Mike? I could join you as soon as we're finished here. She's not hurt or anything."

"Of course." He would miss the doctor from Kenya, but he didn't want Clayton distracted as the college honored him. And there would be videos available after the session.

"Catherine's in the hotel," Clayton said.

"I'll leave messages," Mike said. "Let you know what I can work out."

He walked to the hotel. Catherine stood near the entrance, cell phone in hand, a shoulder bag at her side.

"Where is she?" Mike said.

"Is Clayton coming?" Catherine asked.

"As soon as he can get away from the awards ceremony."

She waved to the doorman for a taxi.

"Mellissa said she was going shopping. But she's at City Hall demonstrating."

He opened the taxi door and she slid across the seat to give him room. She leaned forward to tell the driver to drop them on Grove, near Van Ness. She seemed more resigned than distressed.

"What's she demonstrating about?" he asked.

"Gay marriage."

"She feels strongly about gay rights?"

Catherine shook her head. "She likes the excitement of demonstrating about anything in front of City Hall in San Francisco."

He looked out at pedestrians. "And you approve?" He did not turn.

"It drives Clayton crazy," she said. "But there is no harm in it. She's not hurting anyone."

She got arrested, he thought. But he decided not bring it up.

Goodlett Place was packed with protestors. The driver pointed out a paddy wagon and three police cars.

Agitated people moved in the streets in different directions, like random blood cells bounding off each other, distracted by anger. He followed Catherine, zigzagging into open spaces to make their way to the wagon, where they pushed and shoved people aside to get to the rear doors. A uniformed street cop grabbed Catherine's arm.

"My daughter's in there," she yelled over the shouts, sirens, and shuffle of crowd movement.

"She's been arrested, then."

"I've come to take her home. She doesn't even live here."

"She'll be booked."

"There's no need to . . ."

The cop turned away as two police in riot gear waved nightsticks and dragged up another woman protestor. The cop opened only one of the rear doors; the woman screamed as the three officers stuffed her into the wagon. Catherine couldn't see. She grabbed Mike's arm to pull herself up.

"I can't see her," he said. The wagon doors closed. The policeman banged on the side and it pulled out.

Catherine dialed Mellissa's cell number. She let it ring until it cut to message response. "Call me," Catherine said.

"They've probably confiscated it," he said.

"Where will they take her?" Catherine asked the policeman.

He was looking up the street, and she moved in front of him so he could not ignore her.

"It's a simple question," she said loudly. Now the cop looked down on her as if he hadn't understood. She asked him again.

"Central booking. Pier 57," the cop said.

Mike and Catherine walked to where they had left the cab.

"He's left," Catherine said.

They walked more than half a mile up Van Ness before they found another taxi. When they arrived at central booking, he called Clayton and left a message.

People and cops milled around in disorganized small groups. People smoked and drank beer from cans; a woman gave a lyrical laugh. A youth leaned against a wall and plucked a guitar. He made no real music and attracted no attention. Near the door to central booking the mood was more hostile; protesters under arrest were let out of the wagons and lined up to be photographed before being herded inside a building with aluminum siding. They saw Mellissa and waved, but could not get close enough to shout to her.

"How do I get to see my daughter?" Catherine asked a female officer, who stared blankly. "When she's booked," the officer said. There'll be a list. It might take hours."

"That's not acceptable," Catherine said.

The officer shrugged.

Clayton called. He was on his way, Catherine relayed to Mike. Clayton arrived a few minutes later.

Mike waited outside with Catherine and Clayton for some word that they would be able to enter the station. The crowd murmur was hostile as people found places to sit and stretch, ready to wait as long as needed for news of friends and family.

"I can't believe she'd do this," Clayton grumbled.

"She didn't expect to get arrested," Catherine said.

"It's embarrassing."

Mike pretended he wasn't listening.

"Let her grow up," Catherine said.

"She thinks only of herself."

"You could be a little more understanding," Catherine scolded.

By eight o'clock the next morning, the crowds had thinned. Only Clayton was allowed into the building to stand in a line for information. Mike waited outside with Catherine.

"Thanks, Michael," Catherine said. "I couldn't have done it without you."

"Glad to help," he said. He had stayed because Clayton had asked him to, afraid he might have to leave Catherine alone in an unpredictable crowd if he was needed at the convention. But Catherine had not needed him, or anyone. She remained levelheaded. She was forceful without hysteria. Mike admired her special resilience.

Women protestors wandered out after booking, subdued and exhausted. Most of the men were jailed. Mellissa came out with Clayton and ran to her mother.

"Was it terrible?" Catherine asked.

"We had a ball," Mellissa said.

"Precious Jesus," Clayton whispered to Mike.

Mike shared a cab with them back to the hotel. He rested briefly before he went to his first meeting of the day.

CHAPTER 14

Two weeks after the San Francisco meeting, Angie Picard, the social worker, stopped Mike in the hall between clinics. She wanted him to see a client he'd remember. He followed Angie. She descended the stairs without holding the handrail, her steps controlled and graceful.

She introduced Mike to an emaciated young woman in a chair.

She was familiar, but he was unsure. "Helen?" he asked.

"You operated . . ." Angie filled in.

"Of course I know her," he said. He smiled at Helen Rappaport. Helen tried to stand to greet him but toppled to one side. She smelled of aluminum, and formalin, and overripe citrus. She smiled, gums swollen and red. Her eyes were sunk into her orbits, the eyelid skin tinted with the faint gray of cobwebs.

He felt the urgency of her condition. He was already examining her. Her pulse was up. She wheezed on exhale. Her conjunctiva were anemic, her nail beds white and unhealthy. She had almost no muscle mass, and her skin had patches of erythema and desquamation, some actively infected.

"Look at her snapshots," Angie said.

Helen took snapshots from a business envelope and laid them out on her lap. In one, she stood before her parents' house next to a Honda coupe. "That's a couple years ago," she said.

She offered a color shot, showing her dressed in a yellow pullover that bulged at the waist and hips and gray shorts that pinched her stuffed thighs and exposed muscular calves.

"That was after my recovery," Helen said. "Just before surgery."

On the next page she was a gaunt woman standing next to a vibrant live oak. "About a month ago," she said.

He took Helen's medical record from Angie. It was still plain from Clayton's notes that at her heaviest, Helen was a borderline case for surgery. Mike's consultation note he had sent to Clayton about hesitancy in recommending surgery was not in the chart. Mike asked Helen about her post-op course. After surgery, Helen spent all day in bed except to hobble to the toilet to pass watery stools. Her fever became chronic. She had required two more surgeries for removal of scar tissue and a third to drain an abscess.

He motioned for Angie to follow him into the hall. He closed the door.

"She'll need admission," Mike said.

"On your service?"

"Clayton's been taking care of her."

"She's afraid of Clayton. She hasn't been back for months."

"I'm sure she has another abscess. And she needs nourishment."

"She can't eat solid foods. She vomits."

Mike called a resident for the admission.

"I'll do the case," he said to the resident. "Call Marcel Rappaport. Have him bring Pamela and get here as soon as they can."

"Will the girl be all right?" the resident asked.

"I don't think she will ever be normal again. She could die."

The surgery went well. Mike transferred Helen to the department of medicine and infectious disease for post-op treatment of her infections. Her abscess cultured two resistant organisms that would be hard to cure.

CHAPTER 15

A month later, Mike decided to eat out. When at home, he mostly ate soup, sandwiches, and microwaved frozen dinners, but when he had time, he ate at Pierre's, his favorite restaurant in the Quarter and only three blocks from his house. The chef-owner was Hubert Jarowsky, from Chicago; he was flagrantly gay and had world-class potential as a chef. But New Orleans fit his lifestyle, and he loved being with his friends, relatively un-hassled by society. When asked he always denied any ambitions to expand his place or move elsewhere.

The restaurant, a converted store, occupied a corner and had two street sides of the dining room with open-air arches crossed with wrought-iron railings. He called his restaurant "The Wilted Geranium," but the only place you'd find the name was on top of a single-page menu, churned out daily on a tabletop hand-cranked copier from the fifties. The interior was always dark, with walnut-stained oak wall panels and painted green wooden tables with deep-red tablecloths. Mainly couples, mostly gays, frequented the place. Few heterosexual families were ever seen. No young children were allowed. And not many tourists. Pierre didn't advertise. No reservations were accepted, and disappointed, sometimes angry, people were turned away nightly.

Mike usually sat on a stool at the bar, where there was enough light to read a book or journals. Behind the bar, above the shelf stacked with various bottles, was an eight-by-five-foot framed mirror where he could see everything in the restaurant and much of the street.

"Steven's getting married," Patronne, the bartender, said to a customer a few barstools down.

"He gay?"

"Hell, no. To a good-looking woman, lives in the Faubourg.

Paints."

"Like houses?"

"No. You know. Pictures."

Mike forced himself to not look, to show interest. Patronne was talking about Rosie, he was sure – good looking, lived in the Quarter. *Damn it*, he thought. *Get control.* He did not want to admit that he was even curious about the woman.

He opened a journal, tilting the page to catch the light from behind the bar.

He'd almost finished dinner when he saw Marcel Rappaport in the mirror. Marcel walked straight to the stool next to him and sat.

"I'd like to kill the son of a bitch," Marcel said, looking straight ahead into the mirror. "It's malpractice."

Mike chewed a piece of steak.

"She can't walk more than a few feet. She can't eat anything. Sips everything through a straw. She sweats and shivers. She's had more surgeries than a movie diva. The drugs make her stomach cramp. She shits blood. And she cries all the time."

Mike wiped his mouth with a napkin and pushed his plate away.

"It will take time," he said.

"Don't bullshit me, man. She's gone from a happy, overweight kid to a skinny corpse."

"She'll improve, Marcel."

"She'll never be the same."

Patronne looked over at Marcel. "Keep your voice down. You want something?"

Marcel shook his head no.

"I'm going to take this Otherson guy down. He shouldn't be operating. Did you know there's a support group for patients who've had the fat surgery? Like cancer survivors."

Mike shook his head. "What are you doing here?"

"I need you, Boudreaux. And I don't want that fucker to know."

"I've turned Helen's care over to internists. I'm not an expert ..."

"In fucked-up metabolism? I'm taking him down. No matter. And my lawyer says I need your records. The real ones. Not just what they hand out."

"You have to go through proper channels. Unfortunately that's the law these days."

"I only got some of Otherson's records."

"I saw her for a second opinion about bypass surgery."

"You told the wife not to do it. From the few records we got from Otherson's office, she didn't meet any of the indications for surgery. She wasn't old enough. Her BMI thing wasn't right. She was screwed up in the head."

"All judgment calls, Marcel. Different doctors come to different conclusions."

"Bad judgment. Malpractice."

"Well, you can request my records, there's a form. Medical records will release them."

"I'll need you to testify. To say what you said to Helen and the ex-wife."

"You don't need me. You signed an informed consent. All the complications are listed there."

"Do you think we knew what would happen? Are you crazy? But you knew, man. You told her not to do the surgery."

"I recommended alternative treatment."

"I'm sick of the double-talk. You won't testify for us, we'll subpoena your ass."

"You don't want a hostile witness. There are other experts."

"Not with what you know. You owe Helen, man."

Mike stood and signed his tab, eager to get out, skipping his usual coffee.

"It's not malpractice, Marcel," he said. "And I don't think you'll ever prove intent, either."

"We'll figure out something."

He left Marcel sitting at the bar with his head in his hands. He felt for Marcel, and he hurt for Helen. She should not have been operated on. He knew that. But he could not bring himself to join in legal action against a colleague and a friend. Technically it would be difficult to classify the case as malpractice. It was judgment, mainly, and in parts of the country it would probably meet standards of care. Marcel would get Mike's information, but internal – not public or court ordered – restrictions on surgeons were needed. Quiet, definitive actions. Mike knew he had to convene the task force as soon as possible.

The task force met two weeks later – earlier than originally scheduled. The assistant dean called on Mike to start the meeting; he again reviewed complications, and then presented the case of Helen, without identifying her or the surgeon. Clayton was no longer allowed to attend task force meetings – it was members-only now – but his presence was pervasive.

Over the next hour, a set of indications for surgery emerged that was approved and distributed directly to Chairman McLaughlin for immediate implementation, and that would be presented to the chairs' meeting for official approval early the following month.

Days after the new surgery indications were approved, a quorum of the OR committee met in the faculty library. Seated around an oval boardroom table were three general surgeons and one surgeon each from thoracic, orthopedics, ophthalmology, urology, and colon rectal. As chair, Mike again directed the meeting. "Complications are documented. Results are subpar," he admitted to the committee.

The question now before the committee was Clayton's loose indications, and the now well-documented complications such as Helen's. Seven other patients incapacitated from obese surgery had been documented. "I told you," Janet said.

As usual, Thoracic couldn't stop talking. He reviewed every detail of Clayton's errors, details that had been provided to every committee member before the meeting. He presented a series of Clayton's complications, which he found reasonable when compared to other surgeons.

Mike then meticulously outlined the options – censor, suspension, probation with monitoring, or termination. The majority of the committee felt Clayton could never be rehabilitated.

"No action," Sam the general surgeon said, still loyal to Clayton.

"We have to take action," Thoracic said.

"He's been a solid member of our department for years," Sam said. "He's built the best trauma service in the South. He's integrated critical care. He trained most of us. No action is an option."

"He's killed patients," Janet from Ortho said. "His mortality rate is almost two percent."

"That's close to the national average."

"And 'kill' is not the right word!" Sam said.

"P-l-e-e-z-e," Janet said. "It describes the situation accurately. I can say anything I want."

"These minutes are discoverable," Sam said.

"I don't think so," Janet retorted. "But so what."

Urology spoke. "A good lawyer can discover anything."

"Otherson's made mistakes before. If a patient dies and there were no solid indications for the surgery, it's willful death," Janet insisted.

"'Kill' is unnecessarily inflammatory," Mike said. "Let's avoid it from now on."

Mike leaned over and told the secretary not to redact "kill" in the minutes.

"Let's move on," Mike said. Passions unrelated to the issue at hand might forge an unjust decision for Clayton. He didn't want to argue word choice too long.

A general surgeon spoke. "If we take drastic action, Clayton'll lose his license over this. It will be known by the state. It could ruin him."

"We've known this for months. What the hell were we doing still debating?" Urology asked.

They waited for Mike.

"Action requires facts. Clayton's surgery has been investigated and verified," Mike said. "Errors have been made. Each of us must determine what we think is justified action."

"Termination!" Janet said loudly. "We have facts. You guys stick together like glue. His indications are still loose. And he hasn't gone for training for laparoscopy, either." She looked to Mike. "Has he?"

"I made sure he was scheduled," Mike said. "I know he signed up. At least started. I don't know if he's completed the course yet."

"This is cover-up management, Boudreaux," Janet said.

"I'm Clayton's partner, too," Sam said. "Mike's handled this right." Sam wasn't just supporting a surgical colleague. He didn't like women docs in the OR, especially orthopedists.

"Otherson must be terminated," Janet said. "Has he gone for a refresher course in bariatric surgery for the obese?"

"That wasn't required or suggested," Mike said. "He's nationally recognized in obese surgery."

"Complications are documented. Results are subpar."

"Don't confuse the two issues. The factual report was on obese patients undergoing bariatric surgery, but the complication that precipitated investigation was the use of the laparoscope to do bariatric obese surgery. We don't know if Otherson's been using the a laparoscope, do we?"

There was a silence until Janet said, "That's a technical problem. Has he been using the laparoscope?"

"Yes. With supervision."

"It makes no difference. Complications and deaths have occurred in the obese. More than would be expected," Janet said. "Terminate!"

"I assure you that there have been no serious laparoscopic complications in the past months; we are addressing only the obese surgery indications and judgement; Clayton's compliance with laparoscopic training requirements cannot be considered in our decision. We cannot consider Clayton's errors to be laparoscopic now."

"He's still advertising," Janet said. "It's unethical to misrepresent results."

"You can advertise and still comply with indications," Sam said.

"Give me a break," Janet said. "You advertise to increase volume. Once you've got the patients interested, you increase case volume by lowering threshold indications. Oh, that's never public. But Clayton's been doing it. And it's wrong."

"The ethics of advertising don't apply here," Sam said.

"Just shut up," Janet said. "It's time to take a dangerous surgeon out of the operating room."

"Six months' probation, with continued monitoring of indications, operating technique, and results but no suspension seems severe enough, and provides some credit for past service and success," Colon-Rectal said. "Call the question."

"Motion for six months' probation," Mike said. "Operation only under supervision. Preoperative review of indications. Independent review of results. Reevaluation at end of probation."

"So move."

"Discussion?"

The vote went four to four. Mike had the tiebreaking vote.

"I vote for probation," he said. He knew if he allowed further discussion and a new motion, it could get worse for Clayton, and he thought Clayton could rehabilitate. "Record the vote as five to four."

"I move a unanimous vote," Sam said.

"All in favor?"

Defeated. And the negatives insisted their objections be recorded as their desire for more severe punishment.

By a recorded vote of five to four, Clayton was allowed to operate with supervision as part of the probation. Mike would join other faculty in an official department monitoring schedule of Clayton's cases. All Clayton had to do was improve his judgment, and not screw up.

Mike called Clayton at home immediately. Catherine answered.

"Probation. He can still operate," he said.

"It could have been worse?"

"A lot worse."

Clayton picked up on an extension, and Mike told him the committee's decision.

"I expected better than that, Michael," he said.

Mike had all the requirements of Clayton's probation in place in twenty-four hours. Clayton did two cases on the following Monday. Mike approved the indications and monitored Clayton's performance through Paul, the anesthesiologist. No problems. At least one other surgeon visited the OR twice during each case, too. Mike arranged with the OR to allow Clayton to schedule only with the most experienced anesthesiologists. And he met with every resident and reviewed protocols for cases going wrong.

"What the hell is going on?" Clayton asked when he and Mike were alone in the doctors' dressing room. Mike pulled on his scrub pants.

"You're treating me like a child," Clayton said. But at least he seemed resigned to the probation.

"Everything okay, Clayton?" Mike asked. "I mean outside the hospital."

"What's okay?" Clayton stared. "What in the hell does that mean?"

"Are you having any troubles? Anything at all? I'd like to help in any way I can."

Clayton glared at Mike. "Strange you should ask that."

"I'm chair of the operating room committee."

"That doesn't give you special privileges to pry. I'm not guilty of anything."

A week went by and Clayton continued to operate without incident. At least some confidence returned to his walk and his talk. All the docs on the surgery service began to believe that when the OR committee met for further consideration, Clayton would have a good enough interim record to prove he was no longer dangerous.

CHAPTER 16

Catherine parked in the Omni garage and walked to Rosemary Dayside's studio gallery on Chartres in the Quarter. A bell tinkled as she opened the door.

Rosemary stood on a plank platform supported by a ladder on each end. She was dressed in jeans and a T-shirt, her hair tied back with a strip of red rag, two streaks of paint on her right cheek. She held a palette and a paintbrush and was working on the upper-right corner of an eight-by-twelve-foot canvas of a down-river scene.

"Maybe I should come back," Catherine said, holding the door.

Rosie looked back over her shoulder. "Mrs. Otherson."

"Catherine, please."

Rosie returned to working. "Did you see something you like? There's more in the showroom across the courtyard. The door is open."

"I wanted to talk," Catherine said.

"I've got an area here to adjust the values before it dries. But it's mindless work and I can talk just fine."

Catherine spoke, unable now to see Rosie's face. "It's a pleasant canvas."

"Grandiose, some say," Rosie said.

"The Mississippi has eternal mystery. It deserves a little grandeur."

"My thinking exactly," Rosie said. She carefully laid a wash to prep what eventually would be sky. Catherine watched.

"What's happened to Michael?" Catherine asked.

"We broke up." Rosie glanced at her briefly over her shoulder.

"Really?"

"Right after that retreat for the faculty."

"Was it someone else for him?"

"I don't think so. I've seen him a couple of times but never asked. And no one in the Quarter seems to know."

"You two seemed in love."

"Maybe. But I loved him more than he could love me. That's not a good formula."

"He must have been devastated."

Rosie laughed. "Definitely not that. But he was surprised. He's a good man. He just hasn't fallen in love yet. Or maybe he has and I don't know." She laughed again.

"Do you give lessons? I mean, I'd like to paint. I was an art history major at Newcomb."

"Almost finished," Rosie said. Two minutes later, she gracefully slipped down the four feet from the platform to the floor. She set the palette and brush on a table and wiped her hands on a towel.

"I want to do Quarter scenes," Catherine said. "I love the Quarter, but living uptown I don't come down often. I'd like to do architecture, gardens, street corners."

"Would you like a coffee? I've got a fairly fresh pot in the back. I'm going to have some."

"Au lait, please."

Catherine watched Rosie as she filled Styrofoam cups from an aluminum urn with a spigot.

"I don't teach anymore, Catherine. I don't have the time or the patience. But there's a great private art school up on Magazine, near where the Whole Foods is going in."

"Can I learn about the Quarter?"

"They do a lot of plein air."

"I haven't heard a lot of positives about that school."

"What I've heard hasn't all been good."

"I've had experience in college."

"Watercolors?"

"Oils, mainly. I've painted on and off since then."

"You'll be a natural. Paint on your own here in the Quarter. I can take a look at your work and make suggestions, if you like. And you're welcome to leave your stuff here. I can give you a key in case I'm not around. You could store your canvases, leave your easel. There's usually parking space in the alley."

"That would be wonderful."

Rosie reached into a drawer and took a key off a ring with many. "Here. This is a spare for the door in the alley. Keep it as long as you need."

"I'd like to pay."

"Never. Just send me a potential client or two."

CHAPTER 17

Saturday was the first New Orleans Jazz Festival day of the season. A percentage of profits went to support BonCare health systems. The weather was all sparkling reflections, cloudless sky, and light breeze, and hot enough to produce a light sweat even when sitting in the shade. Streets were crowded with patrons, traffic was prohibited on many streets, bands played on street-corner stages, and you could buy anything – all sold from collapsible booths, wagons, satchels, handbags, even pockets.

The main stage was head-high, a covered platform at the edge of Jackson Square. Speeches asking for donations were slotted between the most popular New Orleans-style piano player and the best rock zydeco band ever to crowd a speaker with too much volume. Introductions by the mayor began at eleven o'clock in the morning.

Musicians for the next set milled around at the edge of the stage. Behind the stage, the Cathedral's spires jutted into the sky. Speakers and dignitaries sat in a line of chairs at the back of the platform. Clayton, who was to talk about the value of his surgery for obese women and children, sat next to the mayor.

Mike stood at the edge of the crowd. He had arranged coverage at the hospital and walked the few blocks from his house to the Square. He'd come to see what Clayton would say about obese surgery with the new restrictions and report to key individuals who would be interested in how Clayton handled himself.

The mayor made introductions and introduced the CEO of BonCare. A hand tugged at his arm. Catherine! He was surprised to see her. It had been months. She looked up at him. "Could we move to the side?" she asked. "Quieter." She smiled with an attractive warmth and intrigue.

He followed her to a quieter spot between two flowering bushes where they could still see the stage.

"Clayton should be up soon," he said.

"He speaks after the chancellor?" she asked. Mike nodded.

They were both facing the stage and kept a few inches of distance between them. She looked to him again.

"Tell me what's going on, Mike? I mean with Clayton."

He didn't look at her. "Clayton's promoting the bariatric service."

"You know I didn't mean that," she said. "That's been there for a long time. Clayton's been difficult to live with. He locks himself in his study. He says he's writing op-eds. He doesn't speak to me. Is it something else at work?"

"People are upset about loose indications, Catherine. New guidelines have been set."

"And the case that went bad?"

"I think that's over. He was almost tagged as impaired, but I think that was unjust. He's still on probation for bariatric surgery."

"Will it hurt him nationally? That's what he worries about."

"I think we can solve it."

The chancellor was speaking now.

"He thinks of you as a friend who turned on him."

"I want him to come through this," Mike said. "He's done a lot for me over the years."

He had not looked at her during the exchange, keeping his eyes to the stage. He tried to concentrate on the chancellor's words, but they carried little meaning for him. He stretched his arms, locking his hands behind his back. He adjusted his stance, his hands by his sides.

He felt Catherine's hand brush against the back of his hand.

The chancellor was describing the historical support given by so many at the festival, noting the fruitful relationship between the university and BonCare.

He felt her hand again, prolonged enough for him to feel her warmth. The contact, at first, gave a sensation of softness, but within a second his mind focused on a pleasant, almost burning tingling. He looked to her; her gaze gripped his, and then she looked quickly away.

His heart was beating hard now. But she had moved away a few inches and did not touch him again.

"Clayton," she said nodding toward the stage.

He was now staring, unaware, unable to erase the feel of Catherine's hand. Clayton had moved to the podium. Now she stepped forward to see better. He buried his hands in his pockets. He studied the back of Catherine's head, her black hair cascading to her shoulders in gentle waves. Clayton droned on. All old stuff. Clayton had not changed his content for a lay audience.

Movement at the side of the stage caught his gaze. Marcel Rappaport wore a dark business suit with a white shirt and tie, and although unshaven, he looked like a participant, or at least an assistant to one of the dignitaries on the stage. He walked slowly and with confidence and few in the crowd took their eyes off the speaker.

Catherine turned her head. "Who is that?"

"Father of one of his patients."

Maybe Marcel would try to speak in protest. There were always demonstrators at these events.

Clayton stopped speaking when he saw Marcel. Marcel pulled a pistol from his pocket, aimed at Clayton and paused. The crowd went silent. Even from a distance Mike could feel Marcel's indecision. Marcel was not a murderer. But he was an angry father who deeply loved his daughter and was capable of seeking revenge. Could he squeeze the trigger?

Clayton was shaking uncontrollably.

Marcel raised the weapon and deliberately fired a shot into the air over Clayton's head.

Two security guards threw Marcel off the stage and dragged him out of view.

Everyone in the crowd talked at once. The mayor went to the microphone to assure all that the situation was under control. He urged Clayton to continue, trying to minimize the disruption. Clayton spoke, but his thoughts were jumbled, and few in the audience even tried to listen, still talking to each other.

Catherine turned to Mike.

"I don't know if I can take much more of this," she said.

Frightened people were leaving the Square. Would something else happen? Chaos increased, but the event was obviously over. Mike took her in his arms for a few seconds, and felt her surrender herself to him. The side of her face was on his chest and he smelled the sweetness of her tears. "It'll be okay," he said.

In seconds, she pulled back and wiped her face. "Clayton needs me," she mumbled. Together they went toward the stage. Clayton had stopped talking but still stood at the podium. Fear had immobilized him. Catherine ran to him. Mike followed.

"Are you all right?" she asked Clayton.

"What did he want?" Clayton asked. He had not recognized Marcel. Maybe he had never met him.

With his attention on Catherine, Clayton was in control again. Catherine and Clayton left the stage together. The Square was covered with police now, and most of the crowd had moved on.

Mike walked slowly back through the Quarter to his house.

Helen Rappaport had died in bed in the night, a suspected suicide from an overdose of prescription nerve pills. Her mother found her. Both the police and the press understood the reason for Marcel's actions, as expert after expert publicly confirmed that Helen had really died of complications related to her surgery. Over the next two days, public sympathy would grow for Marcel. He was charged but was free on bond.

Mike ate out alone that night at Pierre's. He took a table away from the street.

"You no like a place at the bar no more?" Patronne, the bartender, asked.

"Feeling a little low," Mike said.

Helen had been robbed of a future by a health care system that was tripping over its own feet. Helen was special; she had fought back from substance abuse and sexual assault with determination few could match. She'd had a good chance of making it all work. She had not been a candidate for surgery; she was a victim of an unnecessary tragedy. Mike knew he should have done more and swore that never again would a patient die because he failed to act.

CHAPTER 18

Five days later, on a still-dark morning, Mike heard a knock. He put on jeans and went down to open the front door. Catherine slipped in. She had on jeans and a white shirt spotted with splashes of dried paint and linseed oil.

She leaned against the door. She seemed to shrink within herself. Looking at her, he couldn't ignore the enormity of her stress, and he hurt for her.

"My God, Michael," she barely whispered. "I can't go on alone. Clayton hates me. Mellissa leaves the room when I walk in."

"She loves you."

"She doesn't want to go away to school. It's impossible." She held her hands to her face, and dropped to the floor. By bending her knees she turned her back against the door.

She looked deflated, as if her usual essence had been let out. It wasn't her fault her world was collapsing.

He reached for her, but she waved him off.

"I don't know why I came," she said. "It was so stupid. I almost didn't knock."

The still air encased her. She stood back up, sliding against the wall.

"I'm glad you came," Mike said.

"I just don't know what to do about Clayton. I can't make it right. He's always thought of me as an investment. A postage stamp to move his career. But not special. And now, with the hospital trouble, he's turned crazy. He seems on the edge of beating up the world."

He instinctively backed away a step. Catherine was married to his mentor. It wasn't right to go against Clayton. He could see her face cloud with disappointment at his holding back.

"Damn it, Michael. I barely have a marriage." She'd pushed up to full height now, her back still against the wall. "I know you care." She sobbed. "I've fallen in love with you."

In his confusion, he could think of nothing to say. The feeling that he had contained and denied burned with sudden intensity. But he could not confess that he couldn't stop thinking about her. Cheating on his friend and teacher was not right. His upbringing and his religion spoke against it. He refused to let his desire to protect her show, and he forced himself not to move.

"I thought you cared," she said with sorrow and humiliation. "It's so ridiculous. I've never been in love, really. I married Clayton because mother thought he was a fantastic opportunity for a young girl. And I thought you could grow to love a person. And then, when we were at the beach, I couldn't help my feelings for you. You didn't do anything. You were just there. And I could hardly keep myself from you, like I was magnetized."

"It was crazy weekend," he said slowly. "It seems so distant now." He was perspiring under his shirt. His pulse raced.

She went to an overstuffed chair and sat down. He stood near the sofa across from her in the faint light of predawn. They remained silent for a while.

"I've tried to talk to him," she began. "'Clayton,' I say, 'I've got to talk to you.' He doesn't even look up. 'About us.' And he almost yells, 'Not now!' 'Does that mean never?' 'It means not now.' 'When?' 'When you're calm.' 'I've never been calmer.' It keeps on like that, and I shove one of his precious eight-thousand-dollar rose medallion vases off a side table. He doesn't move. But he looks like he's going to kill me." She wiped away tears with her fist.

"I'm an afterthought to him. And when he does think of me, I irritate the hell out of him."

She rose on tiptoe to control her emotions.

He sat next to her on a sofa. "What about Mellissa?" he asked.

She looked surprised. "Mellissa doesn't care. Clayton hates her. He demands her to do something. She does exactly the opposite. They scream and curse. She schemes ways to stay away from home when he's there. I don't blame her."

Mike paused, finding his words. "Clayton did a lot for me when I was in training. It's hard to forget that."

"Is there a chance you care for me?"

He was tense. He stayed quiet and motionless.

"You don't care, I've got no one." She cried.

He could not reach out to her, touch her. He feared losing his resistance; yes, he did want her. "We've got to live our lives as before," he said. "We can't make wrong moves that could ruin us."

She nodded slightly. "Of course," she sobbed. "But you won't go away. I don't think you will ever leave me."

"It must always be secret," he said. "Clayton can use it against me and those who want to prevent OR disasters. He'll say he's innocent and I'm attacking because of feelings for you."

She nodded. "I'm beyond logic, Michael. I'm sorry."

He was suddenly uncomfortable so close to her. "I've got to be in early. I'll get dressed." He went to the bedroom and took a shower. The house was quiet while he was dressing. He didn't call out. When he returned to the living room, Catherine was gone.

For the rest of the day, he tried not to think about her.

Two mornings later, on a Saturday, he was off call and still in bed. He heard a knock on the door.

He descended the stairs to open it; he didn't see her at first, standing back away from the light. She'd been waiting in the rain for some time. Soggy strands of hair kept falling over her face. Her nose was running from the cool air. She wiped her nostrils with a wadded tissue. She took a deep breath to calm herself but she looked flustered and out of control. She felt for his hand without seeing it. He felt her warmth. "Oh, Michael."

He held her hand tightly.

"Clayton's never been faithful, Michael. He doesn't care."

She waited. With the fingers of her free hand, she pushed up the corners of his mouth, one at a time, for a smile. "It can't be wrong," she said.

He tried not to, but he smiled. To release himself was to find a joy. His heart pounded. He took her other hand.

He kissed her lightly on the cheek and gently led her into the house. With infinite care, he treated her with the respect of a priest giving sacrament. She kept her eyes closed. Within minutes, she felt the length of him, and not knowing what the future would bring, she savored the moment of finally being one.

"Catherine?" he said later as the sun came up and they were standing at the door.

"Yes, my sweet."

"Clayton must never know."

She kissed him. "No one will ever know. We can do it."

CHAPTER 19

They met whenever they could, if only for a walk or a few words together. On rare occasions when they could both get away, they went to a hotel in Bay St. Louis or Gulfport. His happiness with Catherine became addictive. He discovered the woman he loved, and each tidbit of knowledge thrilled him. There was no reason or logic to it. Falling in love with a married socialite mother had never crossed his mind – and it would never be accepted by his own mother. Still, he marveled at the inevitability that had conquered his former good sense, and he found his captured state pleasantly humorous. He even convinced himself that no one knew. They were careful to the extreme, and they thought that was enough. But their passion was not easily suppressed, and people at work said he'd changed, that something was different. He told them he'd been working out at the gym more.

Each day was flooded with memories of Catherine's presence. But when he was exhausted, a cloud of source-less apprehension, an embryonic dread, descended on him. He ignored those times as best he could, and he thanked God daily for this gift of a woman of perfection.

Michael, in accordance with OR committee restrictions, continued to assign surgeons to cover Clayton in surgery. He was in a hallway going to clinic when a resident ran up to him.

"Emergency," the resident said.

"OR?" Mike asked.

The resident nodded. "Abdominal aorta. Otherson."

That was damn near impossible. *Goddamn it!*

Mike took the stairs, and within minutes he entered room twelve.

All the staff was as silent and motionless as a snapshot. Only Paul Smythe, the anesthesiologist, looked at him. Paul handed Mike the dead patient's chart. Mike checked the unfamiliar name. Clayton was sitting on the floor, his knees up, his back against the wall, still gowned and gloved.

He could not bring himself to help Clayton up; Clayton would resent the attempt. Mike turned to the staff to begin to clear the room and document everything they had seen or heard.

Within twenty-four hours Mike knew the death was avoidable. Clayton had been operating without his assigned supervision, against the rules of the probation, and posting his case under Mike's name as assistant/mentor without Mike's knowledge.

The hospital administrator gathered a quorum of the OR committee. Two hours later Clayton was suspended indefinitely, finished as an operating surgeon. Only one question remained: Would Clayton lose his license to practice medicine? The state board of medical examiners would decide that. Members of the committee openly wondered what had happened to Clayton, amazed that a man so prominent could fall so far.

Mike went to Clayton's office. Clayton was alone.

"The committee has taken away privileges," Mike said.

"Make you happy?" Clayton asked.

"I wish it hadn't happened."

"I know about Catherine," Clayton said.

Mike swallowed involuntarily.

"You think you love Catherine. But you don't know love, Michael. You don't know about caring and sacrifice. About tolerance and forgiveness. And you can't ever know what she means to me." Clayton leaned forward. "I'm not impaired, Michael. God knows, I've had bad luck. Can you deny that every surgeon hasn't had some bad luck in his career? But if I were really impaired, wouldn't my partner screwing my wife put a little stress on me?"

"That's got nothing to do with the privileges," Mike said. He looked to Clayton for anger, but Clayton seemed strangely resigned, as if he really believed that fate was methodically working against him.

"It's got everything to do with it, Michael. You didn't have to destroy me," Clayton said.

"That's not the way it happened, Clayton."

"I would have given her to you!"

"This committee had no other choice. This was about operating competence. You didn't follow the rules."

"Go to her. Gloat together. I'll work on my life. I'll have plenty of time."

"There is only one issue here, Clayton. Your incompetence."

"Bullshit. There are two issues, and they've never been separate. Your attacks on my career and your screwing Catherine."

Clayton stood up, his hands on his desk, leaning forward. "After all I've done for you," he said.

Mike looked away. "I've never been against you, Clayton."

"Rest your case with God, my friend," Clayton said. "And may you rot in hell."

For weeks, Catherine could not get away from the house. Clayton had become irrational. Once he slapped Mellissa. For the most part he stayed locked in his den. He slept there in his underwear on a sofa. He no longer ate meals with the family, and ordered takeout food delivered. Catherine was afraid to leave, both for Mellissa's protection and Clayton's safety. But she had also consulted with a lawyer who said that in her best interest – and Mellissa's – she could not leave voluntarily, and she should not have any hint, much less evidence – that she was having an adulterous affair. It would diminish her legal claims considerably. He said she should consider herself warned.

CHAPTER 20

A week passed. Mike was on in-house call on a busy night. At three o'clock in the morning, he received a page from the operator that a woman wanted to see him. The operator didn't know who it was. He heard her ask on another line. A friend, the operator said.

Catherine sat in the lobby on one of the sofas with ripped upholstery, her head in her hands. She stood as Mike approached. Her tired eyes avoided direct contact. Her hands fidgeted, and she twirled her car keys on her finger.

The side room off the lobby where machines for snacks and drinks lined the wall had three vacant tables with chairs. Mike bought her coffee out of the machine and they sat opposite one another at a small table.

"Clayton will be back to work," she said. "He's suing the hospital, the state, maybe even you. He claims restraint of trade. Defamation of character. He thinks he can get the court to somehow reinstate him until there is legal resolution. He plans to show up at work and demand a paycheck, and if they don't allow him to operate, it will prove that there's a conspiracy against him."

He had expected Clayton to fight back. He trusted every word Catherine said.

"He can't succeed," he said.

"Oh, yes, he can. He has enough money, and by using the political connections that my father gave him over the years, he's determined to make it work." A facial twitch closed her right eye with irregular spasms.

"I've been driving around for hours. I'm going to mother's," she said. "I came to tell you."

Catherine looked defeated and exhausted. He now knew what Clayton could do to a good woman; Clayton was not easy to change, especially when he was wrong. And he was mean.

"What can I do?" he asked.

"I can't stop thinking about you. I don't know what you can do. I just needed to let you know."

"What about Mellissa?"

"I'm sending her East. No matter what. Mother won't let her stay in her house. She has denied her own granddaughter. Refused any support. I'll have to leave her with Clayton for a few days."

Her eyes moved left and right, up and down. In the fluorescent lights the beautiful brown of her irises seemed washed out.

"He'll never operate again?" she asked.

"He'll find something in medicine."

She turned her eyes away from him. He could not see her face.

"Come to my place," he said.

"I can't. I talked to my lawyer. He says I must never reveal any alienation of affection. I could lose everything."

"They'll argue that no matter what you say."

"Father depends on Clayton for finances. It's been that way for twenty years. He'll not be happy when I leave Clayton."

"We can still live together."

"Clayton won't support Mellissa. He thinks she's useless. And he owes me a lot for all those years. I can't let that go. I'll wait until the settlement."

An old woman and a child walked hand in hand from the elevators to the front entrance. Catherine was crying.

He looked around. A night employee came in, bought a soft drink, then sat at a table and opened a brown-bagged meal.

Mike touched Catherine's arm and nodded to a darkened hallway. He faced her when they were out of sight, self-consciously holding back action to express the desire he felt for her. Finally he touched her, felt her trembling.

"I'll go to mother's," she said. "No one must know about us."

"Leave when he's not there."

"He's always there. Scheming revenge."

"Call me."

"As soon as I can get away."

"I love you," he said.

"Oh, Michael. I wish this could have been easier."

Catherine still hadn't called four hours later. He had no messages on his cell phone or at home. She did not answer her phone. No one was picking up at the mansion.

He drove uptown. Lights blazed in the windows downstairs and up. Catherine's car was in the drive.

Clayton answered the door. "Mike!"

He looked over Clayton's shoulder into the kitchen. No Catherine. "I've come to see if you're doing okay. It's been a while."

Clayton stared. "It's early. But I'm glad you're here. I need to talk to you," he said. He moved outside, brushing against Michael, and closed the door.

"Catherine okay?" Mike asked.

"Of course. I want this to be private."

Clayton motioned for him to follow a few yards from the house.

"I wanted to thank you for what you did the first time in the OR committee. I know you did your best. I'm not after you. But I'm fighting back. I'm suing the hospital, the department, the state board. But I'm not going after you. I told the legal guys no. You were my friend."

Clayton's tone was controlled and flat.

"And I wanted to tell you it's been really difficult with Catherine," he continued. "Hard on her, I mean. She's on the verge of walking out on me. But we've worked it out. She's a great woman. An understanding wife. We've had a heart to heart. I wanted you to know. And she'll need the support of all her friends."

"That's great," Mike said.

"Mellissa will be going away for school," Clayton said. "She's back to almost healthy about her schooling now. I guess Catherine and I will have to be thinking about downsizing. This place is too big for the two of us."

Catherine's face appeared in the kitchen window. She looked

away. She did not seem in danger but Mike couldn't sense her state.

"What do you think about the hospital?" Clayton asked Mike. "I'm sure all charges will be dropped soon."

"How's Mellissa?"

"Like I said. Going away to school. All decided."

"I mean now."

"Great." Clayton walked to the house and opened the door. He called out. "Catherine. Get Mellissa. Say hi to Mike."

Catherine stepped up. Her arm was around Mellissa's shoulder and she pushed her forward.

"See," Clayton said.

Mike started forward to enter but Clayton put his arm out.

"You go on," Clayton said. "I want some production data from the OR. I've requested it. Could you be sure to send it on?"

"Everything's all right?" Mike asked again. He couldn't read Clayton's mood. Was it sarcasm?

"What would you expect, Michael?"

Neither Catherine nor Mellissa made a sign of distress.

"Everything is just fine," Mellissa called. He was too far away to know if her tone held nuances he needed to hear. "Thanks for coming by." The door closed.

Clayton shook his hand. "Let's get together for dinner sometime." He went into the house.

At home Mike left his cell phone active. He was exhausted, but he couldn't sleep. By the time he left for work a few hours later, he still hadn't heard from Catherine, and she did not answer her phone.

Catherine finally called the next day at the office. She was at a pay phone. Clayton had taken her phone away.

"Oh, Michael. I'm so sorry."

"It was a real surprise," he said.

"Clayton and I had this long argument. He threatened me."

"I thought you had decided."

"It's terrible. Mellissa refuses to go to school away from New Orleans. She's got a boyfriend. Now Clayton's convinced she's not his daughter. He says she looks like a stranger. He says that when he proves it, he'll cut me off without a cent if I ever think about leaving him."

"That's crazy."

"Of course. He says my philandering has brought Mellissa's parentage into question."

"Come to the Quarter," Mike said.

"I still have to be careful. My lawyers tell me to document his crazy behavior. I've got a little pocket recorder. I've got to build up my own case. Put this behind me. Even my lawyer says that. They say I shouldn't make any bad judgments now. To ride it out for a while until we can set up a solid reason for leaving. He thinks I can lose everything."

"Call me if you need me."

"I'm afraid," she said.

"I love you," he whispered.

CHAPTER 21

Mike heard from Catherine later at work. She could no longer stand it, no matter the consequences. She had gone to her mother's with Mellissa, but her mother refused to have Mellissa in the house. She'd gone back home; she couldn't leave Mellissa alone with Clayton. Now she was trying to find someplace to live. It had to be close to school and safe.

"Come to the Quarter," he said again.

"Not yet. The lawyers . . ."

"People will know soon enough. And we can manage."

"It's such a risk, Michael."

"You can't stay there much longer."

"I've got to think . . . I'll call you when it's safe. The lawyers say the phones are tapped to trap us."

He returned to clinic but had difficulty concentrating.

Mike arrived home after work the next day at six-thirty. Catherine was pacing in front of his house. Mellissa sat among five large suitcases, her back against the front door.

"Let's get inside," he said.

He unlocked the door and carried in the luggage. Mellissa looked around.

"Where am I going to sleep?" she asked.

"You'll be on the sofa here," Mike said. "We can find someplace better for you this weekend."

He emptied two drawers in a chest and took some clothes out of the closet. "Use that for now." He could store some of his stuff in the rented garage.

Catherine unpacked and got a glass from a cabinet for her toothbrush in the second-level bathroom. Mellissa could use the kitchenette sink. Mellissa stacked her clothes at the end of the sofa in the living room.

Catherine seemed relieved, but Mellissa's face was as blank as a dense fog with no wind. She showed no reaction at Catherine moving into Mike's quarters upstairs.

By the end of the week, they'd developed a sort of routine. Catherine bought Mardi Gras decorations at Walgreens and decorated inside and out. She drove Mellissa to school every weekday morning, then spent most of the day at her lawyers' offices. Most afternoons, Mellissa took the St. Charles trolley and walked home from Canal Street.

Catherine bought plants. Mike now sat in the bathroom next to a two-foot cactus, and woke up to his favorite view of the sky through the French-door windows now partially obscured by a sprawling fern.

The first time Mellissa and Catherine argued, he spent an unnecessary night at the hospital in the on-call room. But he missed his house and the two of them, so he sat them down and insisted on no disputes. They were angry, but sheepish, too, and they were civil to each other when he was around, although he sensed some remaining tension, mostly over Mellissa's going away.

Catherine found a special smile that she flashed more frequently now, thanks to being apart from Clayton. "We wouldn't have survived without you," she said to Mike one night before they went to sleep.

Her work against Clayton was still intense, but not all consuming. Irrational outbursts erupted sometimes. During those times, Mike told Mellissa to understand, and he was surprised that together they could work occasionally to reverse Catherine's pains.

CHAPTER 22

M ike and Catherine awoke after eight one Saturday. Mellissa always slept late when she could – she could fall into deep sleep in seconds, and would sleep for centuries if not awakened, twisting and turning and mouthing unknowable words from her dreams. Mike got hot dogs to go and beer and sodas from a grocery on Esplanade, and he and Mellissa had an early lunch. Catherine had gone to care for her plants in the solarium at the mansion while Clayton was gone from the house. She said the visit was to erase any doubt that the house was still half hers, and that anyway she really needed to get out of the Quarter for a while, something they all agreed anyone needed on occasion.

In a moment of rare togetherness with Mellissa, Mike read journals as she practiced a new pose – for her French Quarter street-mime act – standing straight with arms out in front, dressed like Nefertiti with copper-colored skin and an Egyptian headdress. She looked ready for the tomb journey to the next life. She'd made a small gold-painted platform, two feet square and two feet high. And she'd propped hand mirrors on the sink edge to check the effect. Catherine had never seen Mellissa as a finished product ready for a French Quarter performance and had discouraged Mellissa's costume work as unfit for a young lady. But with Catherine gone, she now worked without inhibition; her pleasure radiated so strongly that Mike smiled.

The act was in three sections: suspension, action, suspension. He watched with growing fascination. At first she stood rigid for up to two minutes, then kicked out with one leg and balanced on one foot, for maybe a minute.

She explained, when he stared, that her boyfriend had a dog

costume. When she was in her regal immobile pose, he came by on all fours and raised his leg as if to pee, and she kicked out, half knocking him over. Then they went into this new suspended pose of him pushed back on one hand and one foot and her about to fall over to the side, a sort of frozen catastrophe. From the way she described it, it seemed like it could be very funny, primarily because she would be so elegant and formal – almost Egyptian divine – in her costume, and then turn into a sort of Charley Chaplin slice-of-life action pose of entanglement with a bladder-filled scruffy dog.

She told Mike that the pose with both of them half falling over was not easy, and they had worked it so her foot on him was anchored in a hidden, hand-sewn costume brace. Once her foot was anchored, the addition of his hand and foot on the ground formed a two-person triangle so they could balance motionless for up to two minutes before crumbling into a heap and passing the can for contributions.

She held the pose twelve times, working for more than two hours. Then she opened a beer from the fridge.

"Don't tell mother," she said. And brought a beer for him. She sat on the couch – her bed at night – her legs sprawled out in front of her. "You don't seem to hate us being here as much as I would," she said.

It was true; he didn't really mind. He had discovered that Mellissa was always thinking, always moving, always questioning. He liked the unhindered vitality that she hid so effectively around her parents. And he began to think he wanted children of his own with Catherine. They would grow, and learn, and be loved. He smiled. It was the first time he had ever had such a thought.

He leaned back in his chair. "Remember that time on Grand Isle when I brought you back?" he asked.

She nodded.

"I misjudged you."

"What's to misjudge?"

"I thought you were spoiled and a brat."

She looked at him. "I am spoiled and a brat."

"Not true," he said.

"Just wait till you get to know me."

She swirled the beer in the can with her arm extended. She took a swig.

"My therapist says," she continued, "I act out to get attention. It's part of my development phase that is too strong. I am not to blame."

"You seem normal to me."

Suddenly she jumped up; she said she had to go.

"Got a date?" he asked.

She packed up her mime stuff, picked up a key to the apartment, and was off to meet her boyfriend. "Stay cool," she said as she left.

Within the hour, Catherine came back. "You two have a nice day?" she asked.

He went to late Mass alone the next morning, and as he came out of the Cathedral he saw Mellissa and her boyfriend in costumes working the crowd with the Nefertiti-and-dog bit. The act was innovative and polished. Their collection can was filled with bills. He added a twenty so Mellissa could see and he looked to her face, but she didn't break her pose. She didn't blink, either. She used eyedrops to keep the pain of a drying, blink-less eye from spoiling the effect of suspended animation.

While Mike was at work, Catherine was still lining up potential witnesses for the divorce or meeting with lawyers. Now he was glad Mellissa still refused to go East to school. She was going to school regularly in New Orleans. Her grades had been borderline average for the last two years, but she'd started studying more, working at the kitchen table some nights until ten or eleven o'clock when he arrived home from the hospital. She was determined to erase any excuse to send her East. She was on her way to the honor roll.

Catherine went to join her parents at the club in Metairie one Sunday for brunch. It had been a family tradition that had become irregular over the past few years. Mellissa didn't like her grandparents, so she stayed home and joined Mike for Mass at the Cathedral.

"You like the Mass?" he asked as they were walking out.

"I don't like when the priest wants God to punish us for not making contributions."

They walked around Jackson Square and picked up a double order of beignets; he had a coffee and bought hot chocolate for her at the to-go window. They climbed the steps onto the levee and found an empty bench with a view of the river. A massive bulk carrier going downstream passed a string of barges going upstream, and they watched together. He loved the river, and he said so out loud. The Mississippi, especially here at the crescent, never lost the power to attract his gaze for hours, like being addicted to the magnetism of flames in a log fire.

He tore open the beignets bag and brushed powdered sugar from his pants.

"School going okay?" he asked.

"I just want to graduate here, not in New York." She looked at him. "Do you ever see your father?" She put her hot chocolate cup down and ran her fingers through her hair; her eyes squeezed shut for a few seconds. Then she broke off a corner of one of the beignets and let her tongue pick up the sugar before she put in her mouth.

"I don't know my father," he said. "He left my mother when she was seventeen and pregnant with me. She never speaks about him."

"Don't you want to know?"

"Sometimes. But for the most part, I live with the fantasy that he was a plantation owner, rich and handsome. He probably wrestled alligators at some roadside reptile farm in Alabama."

"I would have done better without a father. He hates me," Mellissa said.

"He doesn't hate you."

"Mom fights with dad, he calls her a whore. He says she's never turned down a guy. Then he says I'm no different because I have a boyfriend."

She was holding her hot chocolate cup in both hands, now, and leaning forward with her elbows on her knees. The arguments had been a part of her life for so long she seemed fatalistic about it. She stared blankly out toward the river.

"You've done a great job finding yourself these last few months," Mike said.

Swallows darted along the path in front of them, pecking for crumbs.

"I could have used a father who cared," she said.

"He's said kind things to me about you. You must have had good times."

"When I was younger."

"He wasn't around after that?"

"That was part of it. And I don't think he and mother were getting along well even then."

"What would you have wanted him to do?"

"To point the way and say I was doing a good job," she said.

He watched a pushboat maneuver a string of stone-loaded barges around the Algiers point, going downstream.

"For a while, mom thought I was pregnant," she said. "I missed a few periods. Dad said he would disown me."

"What happened to the baby?"

"The tests were negative. It took a long time for mom to get over it. She was absolutely sure I was doing sex, or drugs, or something."

He sipped coffee and stared across the river to Algiers. Mellissa paused with her thoughts, fidgeting with the silver rings on three fingers of her right hand.

"Mother sent me to a therapist. Always I was wrong. It took me a long time to get it worked out." A flock of birds rose in perfect unity from the top of a grain barge like a blanket held on both ends and slowly rolled to air out. "Even now I don't feel good about it. About how no one believed in me."

"You seem to have worked through it," he said.

They sat in silence. The barge with the covering of birds slipped into the shadow of the bridge upstream. Mellissa put her empty cup down.

"Maybe we should start back?" she said.

At the apartment, Mellissa did her homework at the kitchen table. He sat in an easy chair trying to read. But he couldn't forget Mellissa's words.

When Catherine returned from the club, she went straight to the bedroom. No one spoke.

He went into the bedroom and closed the door. Catherine lay on her side of the bed, awake but silent.

"Mellissa's here," Mike whispered to Catherine to keep Mellissa from hearing. "She needs to know that you love her."

Catherine turned. "I made a mistake about the pregnancy. She was going through bad growing pains. And a lot of stress."

"You don't still blame her?"

"No." She said softly. "I mean, the memory is always there. Something happens in life, it doesn't go away. I've told her over and over I was sorry. I think it was too hurtful to really allow forgiveness."

"I misjudged her," he said.

"You've done a lot for us," she said. "We're doing better."

"She doesn't want to go away to school."

"They were about to expel her based on past behavior. I want better for her. And Clayton can afford it."

"She's a good kid," he said. "She's turned things around. I don't mind if she stays."

She looked away. "I'm afraid if she stays she'll go bad. She's angry all the time. This prep school in the East is famous for discipline. She can find herself."

"And get away from the boyfriend?"

Catherine looked at him for a minute. "That too," she said.

He spent the entire next weekend on call at the hospital. Catherine called him at work; Mellissa was refusing to leave for school. Catherine had packed Mellissa's bag, had the ticket ready, and Mellissa refused to go.

He got back to the house Sunday night just after nine o'clock. The door was unlocked. Catherine sat at the kitchen table in a sports bra and workout pants, her bare feet planted on the floor. An open bottle of wine and an empty glass sat on the table.

"It's a disaster," Catherine said.

Mike moved to stand her up, hold her, but she pushed him away.

"Where's Mellissa?" Mike asked.

"I lost my temper."

"What's happened?" He took the other chair and sat across from her, leaving his briefcase by the door.

"She will not listen. It's the boy!"

He stood and opened the bedroom door. Mellissa sat on the bed holding a washcloth to her face. She didn't look up. He closed the door behind him.

"Are you hurt?" he asked.

Mike moved the face cloth. Her forehead and temple were swollen and blue. She had a half-inch cut above her left eye that oozed blood. He led her to the bathroom, sat her on the closed-lid toilet, and found an adhesive strip to approximate the wound edges. With gauze, he made a makeshift pressure patch.

"What happened?" He closed the door and spoke softly for some sense of privacy.

She would not look at him.

"Mellissa. Talk to me!"

A tear welled up in her right eye.

"We are living together in a cramped three-room house. We can't make it if you don't talk!"

She glanced briefly at him then looked away.

"Are you hungry?" he asked.

She shook her head no.

"You *are* hungry!" He took her arm to get her to stand. "We're going to get something to eat."

"I don't want . . ."

"We're going to get something to eat!" he said in her ear.

He guided Mellissa by Catherine.

"Don't go," Catherine said.

"We'll be back. I have my cell phone. Call if you need me," he said. Catherine moved to the bedroom, taking a full glass of wine with her. He'd never seen her take more than a few sips in an entire evening.

Mike and Mellissa walked toward Charters to a po'boy and burger place. He found a booth near the back, away from loudspeakers and with dividers on each side so they were hidden.

He ordered a grilled cheese for her, an oyster po'boy for him.

They sat. Mike didn't say anything for many minutes. Mellissa looked straight into the narrow wooden table between them. She cried silently only once. When their food came, he began to eat. She didn't touch her plate, her hands in her lap below the table.

"It's terrible to feel so bad," Mike said. "What can I do?"

She looked at him before she spoke. "I hate it here."

"But you refuse to leave?"

Mike sipped a beer and waited.

"I'm not a whore," she said. "I have sex. I'm not a whore."

"Your mother gets upset when she doesn't know where you are. Why don't you just tell her?"

She closed her eyes. "I've got a new life. I don't want my parents screwing it up."

"Is it the boy in the act?" Mike tried to look interested and disinterested at the same time.

"He's a senior."

Mike paused. "Why not just tell her? Bring him by."

"She'd go ballistic."

"You like him. She might, too."

"I love him. He loves me. But he's Jewish."

"Don't tell her that."

"He looks Jewish."

"If he's old New Orleans, maybe it wouldn't make any difference."

"His parents are from Cleveland. They live in Philadelphia now. He's staying with his aunt and uncle in Slidell so he can finish school. He wants to be an architect."

Mike thought about that for a while.

"It's the real thing for you guys?"

"He's kind. He's got a part-time job constructing floats at Mardi Gras World. I help him."

"Somehow, you've got to let your mother know."

"She wouldn't do it on purpose. But she'd ruin us." She stared down, her shoulders slumped.

"She wants you to be happy. I know that for sure."

"My mother has lived without love for so long – until you. She thinks old."

Mike ordered coffee. Mellissa declined. After the waiter returned, she leaned forward, both arms on the table.

"I'm spending the night out."

"You've got a place?"

She hesitated. "He's got a friend who has a two-bedroom apartment. His friend travels."

For the next few minutes, neither of them had any more talk.

He finally began, "You know what we were talking about by the river. When you were younger. Your mother loves you. She just didn't know how to handle it." Mike paused. "Your mother needs you. She needs your forgiveness."

"She's had that. She just can't accept it."

The boyfriend was at the door. She stood up. The strong light above and outside the door made his face a shadow. He did not come in.

"What should I tell your mother?"

"Tell her I love her."

He put cash on the table. He stood and paused, watching her walk to the door. Then he hurried to catch up.

Mellissa hugged a dark-haired, wiry young man a few inches taller than she. Mike could see the boy's eyes, intense, but grateful for Mellissa's affection, too.

Mike grabbed the boy's arm, separating him from Mellissa, as the boy tried to twist away but Mike gripped him firmly, staring down into his puzzled eyes. The boy was not afraid.

"What's your intention?" Mike said angrily. "What exactly are your plans for this girl?"

"Don't," Mellissa said.

"This isn't right, Mellissa," Mike said. "This running off, spending nights together without your parents knowing where you are."

"It's none of your business," the boy said.

"Your mother should know," Mike said to Mellissa.

"You're not my father," she said. She was crying.

He let go of the boy's arm. The boy looked to Mellissa with concern and took her in his arms. Mike backed away.

"I'm all right," Mellissa said to the boy. He glared at Mike.

The two left hand in hand and disappeared into the darkness of an alley a few yards away.

Mike stood motionless until a large man bumped into him,

knocking him off balance for a second.

"Sorry, sir," the man said with slurred speech, smiling lopsidedly.

Mike shrugged.

Catherine was asleep when he returned, and she didn't wake when he got in bed beside her. The faint scent of wine hovered over them. In the middle of the night, she poked him.

"Where's Mellissa?"

"She's spending the night out."

"You let her go?"

"More like I didn't stop her," he said.

She fell asleep, turning often and talking in her dreams.

Mellissa came home again after that, but three days later, Mike had been home from work for an hour when Catherine arrived at the house. She had been at her lawyer's for most of the afternoon. Mellissa had not come home after school. They searched upstairs and downstairs for a note.

"She's gone," she said to him.

"I doubt that," he said.

"I know it, Michael. She should be here by now."

"She's probably still at school."

"She's not. I went by there. It's my afternoon to pick her up."

He stood and led her to the bedroom. He pulled out his suitcase from under the bed. He took out his travel bag and looked in a slot in his toilet kit.

"Her money's gone," he said.

"She hid money from me?"

"I gave her a safe place to keep it," he said. "She made it on her own."

He took out a folded note from where the money had been. It was addressed to "mom." He handed it Catherine, who opened it up.

"She's all right. She has a plan. She doesn't want to go away to school." She handed the note to Michael. "She said she loves us. It's the boy she doesn't want to leave."

She sat at the kitchen table and put her head down. "It's my fault I hit her. I lost my temper."

"No one's at fault."

"But I hit her. I've never done anything like that. And now, at the worst time . . ."

Mike held her shoulders, rubbed the tense muscles in her back. "She'll be just fine. There is no one more competent to manage her life than your daughter."

Catherine got up to empty the dishwasher. Then she scrubbed the sink with abrasive cleanser.

"Come to bed," Mike finally said.

"She's a child."

"She's an adult with smarts and a lot of common sense. Like her mother."

"I don't like it."

Catherine called everyone she thought might know where Mellissa had fled to. There were no clues to her whereabouts. Clayton refused to help. She contacted the police and they quickly determined from Mellissa's note that she was not a missing person. Catherine hired a private investigator, who after two months had made no progress. Catherine thought him incompetent and refused to pay him. Mike paid the bill to prevent a lawsuit.

CHAPTER 23

With the mansion in town sold, the house on Grand Isle felt like exile to Clayton. His idle days agitated him. His surgical skills were slipping away, too, like an ice cube melting in the sun. He tried to read journals but couldn't concentrate. He did not play sports, but he'd started taking long walks on the beach. Two days a week he made trips to his lawyer in New Orleans, where they devised strategies. Two investigators now followed Mike and Catherine and searched for evidence that could keep Catherine from getting a penny. And Clayton wasn't giving anything to Mellissa as long as he was alive. Catherine had left – that was her mistake. And he had kicked Mellissa out. The lawyers were shaping up an alienation of affection, as a scare tactic mainly. Christ, anyone could alienate anyone in Louisiana. But they were looking at suing Mike for personal wrong, some vindictive restraint of trade, if they could get that to work. In his mind he wanted to see Catherine wandering in the Quarter, her lover gone, her speech incoherent, wax in her ears and hair under her arms, her toes poking through discarded tennis shoes fished out of a dumpster. The walking dead. That was his fantasy, and it drove him to look forward to the lawyer meetings, and to prod them to look in every crevice for smoking guns.

Although restricted from practice in Louisiana until a decision by the state board, he still had licenses in Mississippi and Alabama. He called a friend he'd known since medical school for a weekend of fishing on the Gulf. With the greatest care, he tiptoed into the subject of hospital-based practice near Columbus, Mississippi. Was there a need? Damned if there wasn't. Was there someplace he could see patients? At the office? Was there a need for bariatrics? Highest obesity in the region. Who cared if the populace fattened up on eating squirrels and possum instead of caviar and duck confit?

He started on a Monday at nine in the morning. He'd spent Sunday night in a motel in Meridian – the drive from Grand Isle was more than seven hours. He saw patients in the office alone, and he missed the bustle of the hospital clinics serving three or four doctors simultaneously. In two weeks, he booked his first surgeries. He lived in a motel when he was working and returned to Grand Isle for weekends.

He was unhappy from the start, irritable with patients and staff. He felt diminished. He was a famous surgeon reduced to a country doctor. The obscurity oppressed him.

He quit forty-one days after he started. A nurse had come to him as he walked out of a patient room, saying, "They won't let me book any more surgeries for you. Your privileges are rescinded."

He went directly to the CEO of the hospital. "What's going on?" he demanded.

The CEO had expected his visit. He handed over the paperwork. The state board had published Clayton's license status in Louisiana, and his errors and status were now also in a national database.

"We just found out," the CEO said. "And you signed a statement saying you had never been denied a license."

"It's under review. I was never denied."

"These are delicate times. I'm sorry."

Screw it, he thought. He didn't like this lowlife; he didn't like the town; he didn't like Mississippi. He left with patients still waiting in the office. His former friend who owned the practice didn't call him, and Clayton never tried to call his former friend, either. He was through with surgery, and it didn't matter a damn what his friend – or anyone – thought.

Back on Grand Isle permanently, he was alone except for chats with waitresses at the diner. He was bored. Television news agitated him; he refused to watch the world deteriorate. Reruns of classic LSU football games entertained him for a few weeks. Then he watched other SEC teams, but soon he routinely fell asleep before the end of the first quarter.

He bathed infrequently, usually walking into the Gulf in his shorts, and then hosing off at the side of the house and sitting in a lawn chair to dry. He enjoyed his drinks, but worried he'd sink into some alcoholic dungeon without a way out, so he paced himself most days, leaving at least three hours between drinks until the sunset.

In his isolation, he became obsessed with telling his story. He didn't type. But he wanted to write, to say things that needed to be said. He would do his memoir. He worried that dictating for transcription would assure mediocrity, so he stocked up on legal pads and pencils with erasers. He'd do better by hand. It would be more intimate.

He set to work on an outline. He blocked out a twelve-hundred-page work in forty-eight chapters. It would take the first twenty chapters, at least, to explore the Otherson family history. Later sections would deal with career and personal development. Then he labored to title each chapter before getting down to business.

But he couldn't wait to get started, so he gave up on the titles for chapters. That could come later.

He started randomly on chapter 38. He labeled it: "Catherine Hebert, MY 'LOVING WIFE.'"

My mother, Beulah Rebennac Cox Otherson, discovered Catherine Hebert among the debutantes that infiltrated every gathering of more than six people in New Orleans. Catherine was my Queen when I was King of Rex. I'd never seen Catherine before then. I knew her father, Gabe. He held state office and was the governor's top advisor — and remained in that position for many years. After Catherine was Queen, Gabe used my money for lucrative oil and real estate deals that would, over the years, give me, and I presume equally him, ten to twenty times the investment. Shrewd Gabe used my money well; I never had major cause to complain at the time, but now I suspect he cheated me whenever he could.

I must say that Iris, Catherine's mother, was already a top hostess in New Orleans when I met Catherine. But she came from low-class origins. Gabe married her just after she graduated from high school in St. Bernard parish. Did she love him? I doubt it. For her, it was a miraculous opportunity to emerge from obscure poverty to the top of New Orleans society.

Gabe paid for every step of her transition to the top. She became polished and memorable. But, as many did, I thought her a little tacky. As Catherine matured, she was living evidence of Iris's climb to power, the recipient of all Iris had learned as Gabe's Pygmalion.

Catherine dropped out of her fourth year at Sophie Newcomb when we married. I gave Iris a blank signed check for the ceremony and the reception. Although they devoted their lives to appear wealthy, it was a sham that everyone with substantive money knew well. Gabe added hundreds of names to the invitation list, but he never paid a cent.

Catherine, in her wedding gown, had a quirky beauty. Her black hair, her brown eyes, and her pert figure did not fit the mold of most New Orleans beauties, who tended toward curvaceous, blond, and ample. But indeed, she duly impressed every male and female with her sharp intelligence and witty remarks. But other than possessing a physical presence that was out of step with most normal Southern beauties, she was, for me, decidedly well chosen. She would carry on the Otherson tradition of exclusive achievement I had always wanted.

When Catherine became pregnant, she was unresponsive, fearing harm to the baby, and after the birth she suffered what I believe we now call postpartum depression. When we returned to my family home – she recovered at her mother's – she established her own room separate from the master bedroom, and she came to me, occasionally, when I called.

I must confess, dear reader, that my objectivity here is a struggle. At the time of this writing, this dear specimen of a wife has left me – for no reason other than her own incredibly selfish needs. She cavorted with my junior partner. As you will understand, my emotions are like rats in a drum-cage.

I must not digress. You can see how hard it is to tell my story when my thoughts are sometimes not my own. But back to Catherine. I *must say she was tenacious. Once she started something, she bit into it like a Gila monster. That may have been a good trait for her, but I think it made her a lousy mother. By the time she came to deal with her child – I say her child because I've come to have serious doubts about whose sperm invaded her womb. She does now, after all, seem willing to accept anyone, even someone as outrageously inappropriate as my friend, partner, and former student. What profession other than surgery demands so much trust? I ask you! But that is history now.*

Catherine lost her tenacity as she raised her daughter Mellissa. (As I say, I'm sure now that girl is not my daughter. She has few, if any, Otherson characteristics. And I plan to gather DNA evidence to prove it so there can never be any claim on the Otherson fortune.) I will say she is a bright child, or at least clever. But headstrong and extremely handicapped. That girl was not born to function in civilized society, and she was unable to listen to any direction that I might suggest to make her life productive. And all the while, Catherine was permissive, permissive, permissive. She came to suspect a pregnancy in Mellissa, never proven, but still, Catherine perceived a breach in her motherhood skills. Mellissa became a constant worry to me, and I never could predict what unacceptable affront she would give next. I will not repeat the wrongs done me here. But you will be able to read these roughly in the chapters on "Beach Time" and "How Education Energized the Othersons." It is enough to know that Catherine and Mellissa did not get along well, and that my life became a purgatory from the content of a happy family.

At this point, he fell asleep.

CHAPTER 24

Catherine's mother, Iris, had a stroke, and for days Catherine never left her parents' house in the Lake District. As there was no one to care for Iris, she began moving her things out of Mike's Quarter apartment. Her mother would not recover quickly.

The second stroke came two weeks later. Catherine found her mother crumpled on the floor at the foot of the open-armed staircase. A full-length oil portrait of Iris in a white ball gown in the fifties, petite and beautiful, proud and defiant in her opulence, was conspicuously displayed on the wall above where she fell.

Catherine screamed for the maid to call an ambulance. She knelt on the floor, wiped the spittle from her mother's face with the hem of her skirt, and then sat supporting her mother's head in her arm. She touched her mother's closed eyelids with her free hand, traced her mother's lips with her forefinger, and silently cried.

How Iris had deteriorated, her face dotted with capillary clusters and brown liver spots on jaundice-yellow skin. She had lived herself into this pre-death purgatory of smoker's cough, high-blood-pressure headaches, and creaking joints, always believing she was above succumbing to the ravages of excess.

Iris could barely function when she returned from a four-day stay in the hospital. Catherine feared the guilt of not doing enough. She blamed herself for not preventing Iris's illness. Instinctively she enslaved herself in excess care to minimize her self-condemnation.

Her mother refused to participate in prescribed rehabilitation. When she did make the effort to walk, she dragged her right leg and her right hand hung down, claw-like. Catherine had set up a bedroom on the ground floor as her mother's room, and had hired two staff to be present twenty-four hours a day. Soon her mother could not make the effort to walk and spent most of her time in bed.

As Iris became almost totally bedridden, she had periods of incoherence where she seemed to retreat into her head to live with good or bad memories, whichever possessed her – some from the past and some she made up. Although she did not seem suicidal, she could not live alone and was prone to accidents. As she retreated into herself, where she felt safe, she failed to perceive real-world dangers.

Gabe, Catherine's father, lived in Baton Rouge now. A campaign was looming for the governor, and Gabe's influence in politics had always made him impressive salaries in election times. But administrations had changed, and he was rarely consulted any more. One Thursday night, he stopped by the New Orleans house. *Strange. He no longer talked to Iris and almost never looked in on her.*

Gabe took Catherine outside to assure privacy. Given Clayton's current problems, and now with the separation from Catherine, Clayton was consolidating his finances – and he was excluding the intricate ventures Gabe had created with Clayton's resources over the past twenty years.

Gabe had built his financial empire on what he thought was a solid money resource. Clayton. And he thanked God it was in the family. But wasn't that in danger!

Catherine could see fear in her father's eyes for the first time she could remember.

"We've got nothing," Gabe said. "Don't expect any more support."

"What about mother?"

"Take care of her."

"With what?"

"Medicare. Insurance."

"It won't last forever."

"Work it out."

"What about you?"

"There's an election coming up. I'll be in Baton Rouge. But the governor doesn't look to my advice anymore. So don't expect miracles."

She stepped back from her father, as if he smelled bad. She had difficulty finding words.

"We could sell the house," she said.

"There's a second mortgage and the market's bad. I have mortgage insurance until next year. But then the house must go."

"I've got less than ten thousand dollars in my account," Catherine said. "The divorce will take a year. Maybe more. Can we sell the cars?"

"You were crazy to leave Clayton," Gabe said.

Her anger flared. *I have a right to flee misery.*

"Clayton's taken back everything," Gabe said. "We were living off those investments."

"Can't you talk to him?"

"I just did. He won't reason. He hates you. You've ruined his career. Humiliated him by screwing his partner."

"It wasn't like that."

"You're pathetic," he said.

She had never allowed herself to admit her father's cruelty. But as it became clear to her how little he cared, she felt alone and threatened.

"Mother needs you . . ."

"Sell the artworks. Try Morton's. Tell him I sent you."

"That will take months."

"Ask your boyfriend."

"He's got nothing. No family money. His mother worked as a medium in Jackson Square."

"Tell her to conjure up a little extra for you," Gabe laughed.

"I could never ask him."

"Afraid he'll dump you?"

How unfair. She was not ready to test the strength of Mike's love by asking him to help support Mellissa's life and her mother's deteriorating health. She would not let money erode what she'd come to treasure.

"I've got an annuity I'll transfer," she said. "But it won't last for long."

Gabe did not return after that. Catherine sold what she could. She dismissed the yardman and the weekly maid – all that was left of the staff. She let the automobiles on lease be repossessed. The returns on the art were not close to their potential value. She paid a little on the house's mortgages when she was threatened by the bank, and she negotiated to postpone payments. But she knew the reality of an eventual eviction.

CHAPTER 25

After Mardi Gras, Catherine made special arrangements for a neighbor to sit with Iris and went to her regular monthly board meeting of the Historical Society. She enjoyed the work and the accomplishment her position represented.

The book that she had written and supervised on illustrations of New Orleans architecture was in galley and ready for the board's review.

Shit. Her name had been removed as author. Instead, credit was given to the board members. She stared down, knowing that the fourteen board members, every one of them, had known – everyone but her. She passed the galley to the next person as the president continued discussion on architectural review plans for the Ninth Ward. When all had seen the galleys, the president asked for a vote of acceptance. Catherine refused to respond to a call for unanimous approval of the galleys by voice consent.

The final item on the agenda was voting on new board member approval and approval of new terms for existing board members, usually routine, since the number of four-year terms was not limited. A new member, Adrienne Lockhart, was approved. Then she and Phyllis Parnell, the two board members up for reelection, were asked to leave the room.

Outside the closed door they waited.

"My name was taken off the book, Phyllis. Did you know about this?"

"The president called . . ."

"Everyone but me?"

"I didn't think that was right, Catherine. I thought she should have talked to you."

"Why? I did the work. I'm the author!"

"It was concern about sales. They thought negative reaction to your divorce ..."

"What has that to do with the board?"

"There was bad feeling about your moving in with the doctor. Clayton has deep roots."

"I'm no less competent as a board member because of my divorce."

"I think you made a mistake, Catherine. I'm sorry."

The president opened the door and with a nod of her head indicated the vote was complete. After Phyllis squeezed by the president to enter the room, the president blocked Catherine when she tried to follow. The president stepped into the hall and closed the door.

"I'm sorry, Catherine. Your term was not renewed."

"It's a routine appointment."

"The discussions remain confidential. But I can tell you everyone honored your contributions."

The president was not looking at her.

"Then why not keep me on?"

"Time for new blood. New ideas."

"Phyllis has been on a lot longer than I have."

The president backed away.

"The vote is final, Catherine, and almost unanimous," she said angrily. "There is no further discussion."

"It's not fair."

"It's what's best for the board and the society."

The president returned to the meeting, closing the door so Catherine had to remain in the hall.

Catherine could not move and tried not to succumb to her disappointment, but she cried.

After her dismissal, without hesitation, she went from the Historical Society to a previously scheduled meeting at her lawyer's office.

"I was fired," she said.

"Just not reappointed," he corrected.

He said he knew why she felt rejected, but that there was no legal action indicated. She must understand.

He turned to "more important" issues of the divorce. She needed the testimonial of Mellissa. They were still in discovery, but a trial date would soon be set. Her case would be strengthened – no . . . her case might be saved – by the willingness of Mellissa to testify about the home situation. It was the only way to counter her leaving Clayton for adulterous reasons.

"We haven't heard a word from her. She doesn't want to be found."

The lawyer said he had a good investigator he could retain. AT Thibodeaux. He could get started tracking her down tomorrow. It could take weeks.

Catherine was sure Mellissa was not in or around New Orleans, and too smart to be easily found. But finally she agreed. She was afraid to ask the cost. The cost of everything had become important to her for the first time in her life. *Why is this happening to me?*

CHAPTER 26

On Thursday morning at 8:39 a.m., Catherine and her lawyer arrived at Clayton's lawyer's offices for depositions. They waited in a conference room. A court recorder and a videographer set up equipment. Her lawyer requested a private room where they might prepare, but when ushered into an unused office he signaled her to be quiet, sure that they were being recorded and videotaped. When they returned to the room for depositions, the opposing lawyer was reading a novel. "Tacky," Catherine's lawyer whispered to her. Catherine waited nervously.

At ten thirty, Clayton's lawyer said Clayton had not shown, and he suggested taking her deposition. Catherine's lawyer advised against it and suggested a new date. "It's a tactic to goad you," her lawyer said.

But Clayton's failure to appear pressed her need for a settlement. For the umpteenth time, she could not repress a fear of failure to obtain a fair settlement. On some days, the fear never left her. *God. I can't go on. I've got to do something.* She decided to try for reconciliation with Clayton without the lawyer.

She did not let Mike know her plans. He would not approve. He'd heard from others that Clayton had been having bouts of mental instability. But she'd come to believe Clayton was her only salvation. He was rich and her husband. Mike had almost nothing in comparison, and together they had only their love for each other.

For her lawyer, she had indexed facts from thousands of papers and drafts and notarized depositions spread out on the floor and marked with color-coded tabs, as if the quality of intense organization would save her. At the moment she climbed in the car for the trip to face Clayton, she forgot almost all the documents she had carefully collected to convince Clayton to be human. She took the SUV, the only thing she still had that he owned.

The drive to Grand Isle was rote, but the once-comfortable world of southern Louisiana was now unfamiliar, almost bizarre. Twice she stopped by the roadside, ready to turn back. She dreaded confrontation with Clayton. *Damn it. I've got no choice!* She drove on.

The sun pinpointed patches of still water; the brown grass on the verge of the roadside was so dry it was almost transparent; lush and green year-round foliage on the land seemed suspended in its chlorophyll cycles. She parked on the street. The driveway of her once-loved beach house seemed unwelcoming.

Thank God Clayton was there. He watched her approach, and opened the door to stare without greetings.

"Clayton. I need to talk," she said. Now that she had arrived, she brimmed with shaky determination. "Let me in." She brushed by him before he could react.

"Sit down," she said, buoyed by her decisive entry. He didn't move. She chose a hard-backed wooden chair for herself. "Sit," she said, pointing to an overstuffed chair. They would be at each other's eye level this way. He complied without speaking.

"Do not cut me off," she said. "We built a life together. Part of *your* success is *our* success."

"No," Clayton said.

"I haven't asked for anything."

"It's done," he said.

She decided to speak without hint of remorse, without contrition.

"You can make it right, Clayton. I deserve that. You need that too," she said forcefully. "Look at you. A hermit, selfish and alone. Your life is a wreck." *And you're thinking only of yourself,* she did not get to say before he interrupted.

"I marvel at how happy I am. I am ecstatically happy." The pulsing of his neck vein slowed. "To finally be rid of you. And that child."

"She's yours. Love her as you once did." But her confidence had fled. He had no compassion for her distress. His eyes blazed with a hate that seemed unfathomable. He was consumed, and he was blaming her.

"Nothing," he said. "You're wasting your time."

Suddenly the inevitable failure of her visit loomed over her. Her life was a house of cards, each support point only touching, never fixed, and any height or width achieved was always in jeopardy. "Please, Clayton." *I planned to never plead.* "I need the chance. Do it for me."

Clayton remained silent and impassive.

"You're evil," she said. "I love someone who loves me, Clayton. Someone who has the gift of loving someone else. You'll never know that. And for that I feel sorry for you."

How condescending that sounded. *Good!* But then her confidence slipped. Did she have any right to criticize him? Maybe she was not the prize of a wife she thought she was. "I'll take you to court. You hit Mellissa," she finally said as forcefully as she could.

"I slapped her once. That's hardly abuse. And she's not mine."

"You'll never prove that."

"Not one lawyer I've consulted believes you'll get anything if I get the right sample."

"You'll find nothing."

"DNA can reveal wonders."

"You're pitiful." She rose with deliberate slowness.

"You're not yourself, Catherine. Have you sought help? From a doctor?"

She strode to the door with as much dignity as she could gather. Her face hurt with tension. She slammed the door behind her, climbed into the SUV. At least she still had that.

She drove in fits and starts. Twenty-five to eighty-five to fifty, but never stopping, taking random turns, crossing the river more than once, slicing through cane fields on narrow two-lane roads, blasting the piercing horn at country bikers and the rare cowering pedestrian.

The sun vanished. Dark clouds rolled and billowed. Raindrops at first spotted the windshield, then sheets of water splashed across her vision, too much for the wipers to handle well. The side mirror images disappeared in squiggles of water. She wept, at times out of control.

She was at the ramp to the Huey Long Bridge and tailgating a slow-moving small car. A brake light winked. She had no view over the side of the narrow bridge, only gray turbulence. Near the top she sped up, then raced on the down slope. The winking light disappeared for a few seconds. Her foot pumped the brake before she jammed her foot down. The brake light was inches away. She yanked the wheel to the left. Metal scraped on metal, she was upside down, hanging in her straps, then right side up – jolts and accelerations. She was upside down again. The world went dark.

From information on the car registration, the police contacted Clayton within minutes, before Catherine was removed by ambulance from the accident scene.

"Michael," Clayton said. Mike recognized his voice on the phone. "Catherine's had an accident. She's coming to the ER."

"How bad?"

"I don't know."

Mike wondered if a bit of concern had seeped into Clayton's voice. He broke the connection and cancelled a minor outpatient procedure. He was at the ER when Catherine arrived twenty-six minutes later. She was bruised, but without serious injury.

He called Clayton. "She's okay."

"Who gives a damn," Clayton said, now without a trace of concern in his voice.

"I just thought you should know."

CHAPTER 27

Mike visited Catherine at her mother's whenever he could. He was convinced that if she could piece together her pride, she would return to their living together in the Quarter. He wanted her with him.

He believed that Clayton still might listen to reason. The recent barriers that had been forged between him and Catherine might be impenetrable, but maybe Clayton – who had taught him and with whom he had worked with for years – might listen to what Catherine was going through. Clayton had sent requests to him for documents. Mike had reviewed the requests with the hospital lawyers. They filtered what they thought they could not withhold, and Mike volunteered to take the material to Clayton.

He drove to Clayton's beach house unannounced a week later. In an envelope he had copies of selected surgical schedules, memos, and letters – a lot of what Clayton had requested.

He got out of the car. Clayton sat shoeless in an aluminum folding chair on the front yard, drinking a mixed drink without ice from a water glass. He was shaven and had a fresh haircut. He had lost weight: the loose skin on his legs had lines around the knees and metatarsals showed under the skin on the tops of his feet.

He handed Clayton the envelope. Clayton set it on the ground and stared ahead without comment.

Mike took a chair that was leaning against the house and brought it back where Clayton was sitting. He unfolded it and sat, leaning forward.

"You know, Mike, I think you had some points about the gastric bypass cases," Clayton finally said, with no hint of malice. "The more

I look at it, I do think we got a little out of control."

"We've got new guidelines," Mike said, not looking directly at him. Guidelines that were established and accepted by the other surgeons after Clayton was barred from operating.

"I didn't want to talk to you," Clayton said. "But I figured, what the hell. You may be screwing my wife. But we had a lot of good years, you and I."

Mike leaned back, feeling there must be something he could say that would help Catherine, but without confidence that he could find the right words.

"Catherine still at your place?" Clayton asked.

"No. She's taking care of her mother."

"Iris is one crazy witch. She deserves hell."

"She is not doing well."

"I'm glad," Clayton said.

Mike paused. "We never meant for it to happen," he finally said.

"That's bullshit, Michael. If you never meant for it to happen, it never would have happened."

"Catherine didn't go against you. It wasn't like that."

"You went against me. Only you could have destroyed my career. You were my student, for Christ's sake. You owed me. Your brain has rotted."

"I'm sorry for what happened," Mike said.

Clayton threw up his hands. "But not sorry for what you've done. My God. You want money, don't you! You think I'll forgive her? I won't forgive her. She'll never get a cent. Even if the court gives her a little compensation, I'll tie it up so she'll never get her hands on it."

Mike had heard Catherine's dreams of a settlement, a huge lump sum and hundreds of thousands every year.

"You've crushed her," Mike said.

"You're the one who promised her eternal happiness. Deny that!" Clayton sank into silence for minutes. He refused to look at Mike.

"Who's paying the legal team?" Clayton finally asked. "You?"

"She doesn't have a team anymore."

"Hah. I ruined Gabe, you know. His money's gone. The son of a bitch."

"Maybe Catherine's mother has some."

"She's white trash. Gabe married her before she was out of high school. That whole family is shit," Clayton said. "Gabe is one pure asshole. Iris is a witch. And Catherine is an adulterer. Pure shit."

"I think Catherine will try to make the point that you mentally and physically abused Mellissa."

"She's probably not my kid. I'll prove it, too. Once I get the right DNA."

"Don't fake it."

"I'll prove it, Michael. Tell her that. No matter what." Clayton hands twitched with his agitation. "I'll get the proof and she won't get the house, either. No part of it. It closed months ago," Clayton said.

Clayton descended into silence again. His breathing was labored. Mike watched him for some sign of contrition.

"She was good to you . . ." Mike began.

"She screwed you . . ."

"You ignored her."

"I loved her," Clayton said.

Mike sought the right words to ask Clayton to reconsider – to think of Catherine. But Clayton went into the house. Mike sat for a few minutes, irritated by his failure to gain anything for her.

A shot rang out, the sound of a bullet, or maybe he had just imagined hearing the bullet. It startled him, and he hit the ground. From the door, Clayton fired another shot.

"Get out," Clayton said calmly, "before I kill you." He fired again.

Mike stood and walked slowly to his car. He would not let Clayton bully him. Even if Clayton was insane.

CHAPTER 28

"Clayton, honey. Ain't see your little red touche in a coon's age." Crystal stepped out the trailer door and sat on the wooden steps with her bare feet on the grass.

"You got time for me?" Clayton asked.

"You shoulda let me know."

"No one answered."

"Well, my old cell phone was disconnected. You been away too long. Busy till after seven."

"I'll grab a bite 'till then. Fanny's still open?"

"Doing burgers on an outdoor grill, but you gotta ask for 'em and pay extra."

He turned back toward his car.

"I take cash only, Clayton," Crystal yelled. "Nothing on the cuff anymore."

He sat in his car. He could see Crystal peeking through the curtains that covered the small window that he knew was above her bed. Was someone in there? He wanted to see what her other guys looked like. *Screw that.* He'd never be jealous of a john with a whore as worn out as Crystal. *Shit.* What did he really care?

And her price was too high. Well, maybe these guys paid nothing and were probably butt-sore from riding a tractor in a cornfield. Wouldn't that be an asswipe? Fucking rednecks getting it for free.

Crystal stepped out of the door and waved for him to move on.

To hell with her telling him what to do. But she kept waving and then started toward him. He wouldn't let her yell at him. He didn't give a damn who she fucked. He cranked up the engine. He'd get a bite to eat. Come back.

He took two bites out of a cheeseburger done on the grill. Tasted like fat-soaked surgical gauze. The fries drooped like earthworms. He ate some Oreos out of a vending machine and drank Southern Comfort straight, sitting in a corner at a linoleum-topped table. The hard wooden chair's horizontal slats dug into his back so hard he had to lean forward.

At seven he went back to Crystal's trailer. A note was taped to the door.

WonT Be BAcK til late oN.

"Late on." What the hell did that mean? Fucking illiterate. Anger surged through him. How could she blow him off? He was more important than any man she'd ever laid. Goddamn her. He wanted to destroy her. Swat her like a fly so she'd be lying on the ground with her arms all crooked and her head twisted and her pelvis flattened out and her skin all crisscrossed with cuts from a good old-fashioned metal flyswatter. He'd shovel her up and put her in this stupid tin can of a trailer and burn the fucker to a handful of ashes . . . with her in it and no trace!

He breathed deeply a few times and his heart slowed. He got back in the car, drove out onto the two-lane road, pushed the accelerator until the speedometer glowed eighty-five. He drove to nowhere at first. When he hit the interstate, he headed south to Algiers. His mind was filled with a faceless woman, naked and crying.

In Algiers he drove to a two-story house, to a whore who had been in business for at least twenty years. A favorite with some cops, too. Three rooms in use upstairs, and two in the back on the first level.

Madeleine was in her mid-sixties and handled up to five or six girls. She always wore an off-the-shoulder black ball gown. He'd never seen her with shoes on, and she never wore jewelry. Her black hair was long and uneven, streaked with gray, and probably felt like wire.

She looked at him with total recognition, even though it had been a couple of years. She didn't say anything – she'd never been big on talking.

"What you got tonight?" he asked.

She stayed spread out on the two-seater sofa. She was watching some old movie in black and white on the TV. She was drinking Diet Coke in a glass without ice, empty cans on the floor around her.

"Ruthie or Tammie Fay."

Neither his favorites. And probably worn out since he last saw them.

"It's two hundred for Ruthie now," Maddie said.

Outrageous. Last time was twenty-five bucks at most. She was scamming him because he was a doctor with a car that wasn't thirty years old. But his urge needed tending, and he wasn't about to try to bargain with Madeleine, who never engaged in discussions of any type. She was the master of two-word sentences, three sometimes, and nonexistent paragraphs, for Christ's sake.

"You got little Pattie in house?"

"She dead. Take Ruthie."

Ruthie had on an Alice in Wonderland white dress with lace that came down to mid-thigh, short sleeves, and a V-neck that showed breasts with angry red pimples and scabby skin. She undressed. She had nothing on underneath the dress. She sat on the bed, her feet on the floor, her knees apart to show him what she had. It looked worn out, scraggly. There were red splotches in the crevice of her thighs.

"What you want?" she asked.

He stared at her. Anger rushed through him like a death-star explosion. He hated her shit-brown eyes. Her hair matted like she'd been hibernating in a cave for the past month, her breasts sagging, one nipple gone with a ragged white scar in its place.

"Is that what you paid for? Lookin'?" she said.

He hit her as hard as he could with a closed fist in the side of the temple. He felt a crack, or maybe it was just her neck jerking. She screamed and he punched her full in the face. He stepped back, suddenly calm and light as if he were on a wispy white cloud. She slumped to the floor. As her head cleared, she tried to stand up. How dare she! Trying to stand when he felled her, like a dead tree. Anger surged again and he kicked her in the side. A rib cracked, he knew the sound. He felt like grinning, swept with satisfaction.

She reached for him as if he might rescue her from her wretched life. Anger consumed him. She got to her feet and he shoved her toward the window. The glass broke easily. She was still facing him, her face distorted with horror as she began to fall, her hands flailing at the shards of glass at the window's edge as she fell back, her feet elevating then disappearing. He heard the plop and a muffled scream as she hit the ground twenty feet down.

Maddie opened the door. Her bare feet gave her a silent, ghostly glide. Her eyes were hard black as she raised a pistol with both hands. "You shit." She fired once. He felt a spike of pain in his left knee as he went down. His vision failed; he could barely make out Maddie bending over the windowsill. Clayton thought he saw the bulk of a man come through the bedroom door as he passed out from fear he was going to die.

CHAPTER 29

Clayton avoided Father Dupont's gaze. Father had married him to Catherine, but he was retired now. He sat in a plastic upholstered chair with chrome pipe arms and a sloping back that was, at the closest, eight inches from Father's ramrod-straight back. Father held a black Bible as big as a cereal box. A red silk red page marker half an inch wide was attached to the spine at the top.

Why would Father visit a lapsed Catholic whose wound was serious enough that he'd never walk without a limp, but far from life threatening? Jesus, Father wanted to save his soul. Not him, he was probably beyond saving in Father's mind, but his soul. *That's why he's here, I'll be a sort of a generic notch on Father's soul-hunting rifle.* Father was probably attracted to how he got here, in this private room at Oschner Clinic, after being found abandoned, half-dead, and in shock from blood loss from a leg wound, in a strip mall near the lake. At University Emergency he had told no one his story, not even his doctors. And his prominence as a physician had fueled wild, curious stories in the *Times Picayune* and on talk radio that had increased in incredulity over the last three days. He had refused to speak to the press. He had refused colleagues' visits. Even Catherine had come. He had let her come in. He was on the verge of tears, immersed in a heavy ache in his leg that shot bolts of searing pain up his leg when he tried to move. She was unmoved. *She thinks I'm faking it for her. Bitch.*

"What happened?" she asked. That was what she cared about. Solving the mystery of his injury, *not* about him. It had *never* been about him.

He had turned his head and stayed silent.

"What can I do?" Catherine had asked. "Mother is ill."

"A curse on her."

"Oh, Clayton. Do we need to be so cruel to each other?"

He moaned with a surge of pain. She must have taken it as a response to her talking about cruelty. She touched his hand and he took it away. "Cruelty, my pet," he managed to say through clenched teeth, "can only perceived by those who listen and care. *I do not care.* You are beyond being able to be cruel to me. I've had too much!"

"I've heard nothing from Mellissa. I don't know where she is."

He laughed. The pain had eased a little. "I still doubt she's mine, you know. Can you deny your whoring? All those extramarital fucks? And the girl never had my disposition. She has your eyes. I'll give her that. But not one feature of mine."

"She's yours. And she loves you." Catherine's voice turned harsh with reprimand. "I was never unfaithful."

"My God. With the man I coddled?"

"To be the best."

"In fucking his partner's wife," he scoffed.

Her voice turned soft. "You're not thinking straight," she said. "Is it the medication?"

"Bullshit," he said. She sat for a few minutes as he seethed in silence, and left.

Father Dupont closed his eyes as Clayton remembered Catherine's visit. He might have been praying, but his lips didn't move. Silent prayer, maybe. Or just tired.

Father opened his eyes.

"Catherine is concerned for your health," Father said.

"Blasphemy."

"Pray with me, my friend."

Clayton said nothing. He suspected Father needed to satisfy his curiosity. Clayton believed he would take any confession and shout it to the world. That was the priest he had become. A gossip. Loving the spotlight. Such a "man of God" would never fool him. Never.

After a long pause, Father said: "There was a girl with you when you were found. Sixteen years old. She had cuts over her body and a lung punctured so she was barely breathing. She was sick, anemic, and sexually abused."

"Not by me, you heretic."

"She says her name is Ruthie. But nothing more. She's frightened. I thought you might know about her family, or who we might call to take care of her."

"I know nothing."

"I don't believe that."

"It's none of your business, you fraud."

"That child's welfare is my business, Clayton," Father said with sharp anger.

Clayton had assumed Father was here for his salvation. But for Ruthie?

"Get out, you charlatan."

Father prayed.

"I don't need your prayers."

"Please tell me what you know about the little girl."

Clayton laughed. "When the apocalypse commences, my good man."

"God forgives you, Clayton. I'll come back when you're feeling better."

"You'll be wasting your time."

Clayton went to the beach house on Grand Isle a week later. He could care for himself, and a nurse made daily house visits to attend his leg wound. He hurt, but had taken himself off all medicines but the antibiotic. His moods were sour, and he still blamed Catherine and Mike for precipitating his fall from grace.

The pain fatigued him. He could not read for enjoyment and spent most of his time mindlessly watching whatever appeared on the TV channel he never changed.

At night he abhorred the silence, and bought a sleep box that made sounds of waves lapping some mystic shore. The image of Ruthie falling through that window would not leave him. Even in his dreams he saw her, usually reaching out for him. Night after night. The images grew sharper, washed with red and white against black and brown. He could see the black holes of her wide irises in the thin rim of her washed-out brown pupils. And he began to hear the sound of her hitting the ground. He would wake up sweating, unable to go back to sleep.

He was restless during the day, walking in circles, dragging his leg. Finally he called the hospital. Ruthie had been sent to a Catholic charity house for homeless children. He drove there.

The nun said Ruthie was still weak and spent most of her time resting. He sat in a wooden chair, staring down at her, asleep on a narrow cot. It was hot, and she had no covers on.

The nun left after a few minutes, deciding that he was harmless.

He watched Ruthie's breathing, shallow and raspy. It had a tenuous echo to it. Her face was covered with stitches still dotting pink and mauve healing scars. Occasionally her eyelids fluttered, as if in response to some inner threat or fantasy. Her skin looked better, but her hair had been shaved and was now only half an inch regrown. He was afraid this new image of her would now come to haunt him. He looked away. Unable to move. Not knowing what to do.

Ruthie woke up. She saw him and screamed, weakly, but as best she could.

The nun rushed in; she had obviously been waiting outside the door.

"It's all right, child. It's all right."

Clayton moved back toward the door, unable to turn away until he had backed into the hall. The nun blocked Ruthie's sight of him, as if she knew Ruthie's dreams were already stuffed with him and a new image would invade her world even more.

"Maybe you should leave," the nun yelled at him without looking, but he was already limping down the hall toward the exit.

He had hoped a visit to Ruthie would erase her from his tortured nights. But there was no relief.

He called his lawyer and set up a trust fund for Ruthie. He instructed the lawyer to provide for improved medical care from a pediatrician and a plastic surgeon he had worked with for years. He arranged for a set sum to be given to Ruthie or her guardian every month, the amount to be adjusted to market value fluctuations every six months. And he gave a donation to the Catholic home, enough to cover their campaign goals for a new wing to their facility.

Then he waited for the night, to see if his visions would fade and allow him to rest.

CHAPTER 30

Catherine was alone with Iris now, with the servants gone and few visitors. Iris had become sensitive to light and insisted on drawn shades and lowered rheostats.

One weeknight, Catherine was reading in an armchair next to Iris's bed. Iris slept fitfully.

Something fell in the yard. She looked up and turned out the light. Her eyes adjusted. The silence seemed more intense. She went to the window, staying to one side to not be exposed.

"Oh, Jesus," Iris yelled out.

"It's all right, mother."

"Mother of God." Iris retreated into herself, forgetting what startled her.

The quiet returned. Catherine held her breath. She heard someone on the drive. She moved quickly to the front door and looked out a side window. She opened the door.

She saw a man. He was at the end of the drive. He hobbled out into the street, leaving the gate to swing open. She saw no details, but she was sure it was a man. As he half-ran away, he seemed to limp.

The police found a plank propped against a fence near the garage. They thought the intruder had used it to better see into the house. They canvassed the neighborhood, but found no one.

Early the next week, Catherine visited her lawyer downtown on Baronne Street. She came out of the building and walked toward her car. She felt an odd sensation of being the object of someone's interest. She stopped and turned, looking behind her. No one seemed suspicious, although there were many people on the street at that time of day. She started again. When she reached the intersection, movement to her right caught her eye. She saw him. He stood still next to a sign pole. He was scowling at her, as if deranged.

"Clayton!" she yelled. He was too far away to hear. She started toward him. He wore clothes from the beach: chinos, Dockers without socks, a pale yellow polo shirt.

Fifty feet way she stopped, unsure of his intent. His face had not changed. He seemed without emotion. His arm leaned against the pole, holding on with his hand just above his head. His smile held no recognition, although he had not taken his eyes off her. She could feel those eyes, engaging her as if she were some dead prey to be killed for the thrill of the hunt. She froze. The menace overwhelmed her. How stupid, she thought. He wasn't threatening her. But he was there. Not accidentally. *But why?*

"Clayton," she called to him. "Why are you doing this?" But he had already begun to move away.

She reversed her direction, and, controlling the panic, walked to the garage. Twice she looked back. He did not follow. Once in her car, she locked the doors and sat, trembling. She could not move for many minutes.

The next day she bought a gun, and took instruction for four sessions on how to care for it – and use it.

CHAPTER 31

Catherine had had no word from or about Mellissa. The investigator recommended by the lawyer, AT Thibodeaux, continued to search for her, reporting to the lawyer. Thibodeaux had talked to Catherine only once, but he called her directly from Maine on a Friday, and said he had found Mellissa. He would wait until Catherine could get there to bring her back. "Can't you arrest her?" Catherine asked.

"She needs family," Thibodeaux said.

Catherine called Mike. "I can't leave mother. Clayton doesn't care. Father refuses to come back from Baton Rouge. Would you go?"

"You should go, Catherine. It would mean a lot to Mellissa."

"I can't, Michael! Mellissa likes you. More than she does me sometimes. She'll listen to you. Bring her back."

"Does she want to come home?" Mike asked.

"I have no idea. But I can't worry about her living homeless. And the lawyers need her deposition. I have to prove a good reason for leaving Clayton, or he could keep everything. I need Mellissa to tell the truth about him."

Mike was on backup for Saturday only, and he got Peter Ravenel to cover.

Mike called Catherine's lawyer. "Pay the investigator to bring her back," he suggested. But the lawyer didn't want her arrested locally in Maine on shaky charges to get her back to Louisiana, and have Mellissa appear as a hostile witness. That wasn't in Catherine's best interest.

⚜ PART THREE ⚜

CHAPTER 32

Mike flew to Portland, Maine, and rented a car. A foot of fresh snow covered the ground; the roads had been recently plowed. Many roadside businesses that catered to the summer tourists were boarded up, the snow around them unmarked by human footprints. On side streets, salted surfaces had iced over and turns in less-often-used areas were treacherous. Mike sat across from the investigator AT Thibodeaux, who wore jeans and a new-looking sweatshirt with a Harvard logo, just after twelve thirty on Saturday. They were in a booth in a Pizza Hut off I-95 in South Portland.

"I got her," Thibodeaux said. His voice had the rasp of steel on concrete, his Cajun accent strong enough to quickly annoy. His dark, cold eyes fixed on Mike.

Mike fingered a menu clamped in a metal holder on the table as Thibodeaux explained that Mellissa and the boyfriend lived on an estate-owned, rented farm with eight or nine adults and four young children, all tenants in a commune setting. She threw pottery with at least two of the other women and one of the men at the Pottery Connection on Route 27. They made decorative and useful items and sold some on the premises, and during the winter, many popular designs were shipped out to retailers or sold through mail order. The boyfriend was working on a lobster boat in season and as a waiter in a Wiscasset restaurant. Thibodeaux's report was complete and efficient. Nothing was in writing.

"You talk to her yet?" Mike asked.

"No talk. She fly like bird on wing, man."

A waitress took an order.

"I want to see her as soon as possible," Mike said.

Thibodeaux scratched the side of his head and frowned. "We got time, man. She work until five. It is no good to take her at work."

"The last flight out is at eight thirty tonight, to Boston to connect to New Orleans. I checked," Mike said.

"You best to make her go easy and slow."

The waitress placed glasses of water on the table and laid down utensils wrapped in paper napkins.

"It shouldn't take long," Mike said. "Let me talk to her."

"She afraid, *mon ami*," Thibodeaux said. "She disappear." Thibodeaux laid out a plan. He would restrain Mellissa if he needed to. Take her back to New Orleans in the back of a rental car. Mike again rejected force.

"I can reason with her," Mike said. "I think I can convince her to come home, at least for a while."

"Plane no good."

"I can talk to her."

Thibodeaux was still unsure, but finally agreed to let Mike approach her alone. They would take two vehicles to the farm where she was living. Mike would approach the house, and Thibodeaux would wait out of sight on the road, ready to follow if she made a run for escape.

Mike left his car unlocked. The house was old New England frame with white clapboard and green trim. The late afternoon sun glinted on the iced edges of the roof. Leaf-bare tops of tree skeletons clustered behind the house in a colorless frame to a dormant landscape. The rusted iron knocker wouldn't move, and he used knuckles on one of the upper panels. The thick door muffled a man's urgent voice, then a woman's, both unfamiliar.

He knocked again. A rear door slammed shut. The front door opened.

A small, muscular youth faced him, his feet planted, his shoulders squared. "You're not welcome here," he said, his voice quivering with anger and apprehension. He was Mellissa's boyfriend. Different clothes. New haircut.

"I've come to see Mellissa," Mike said.

"We knew it would happen."

"I don't know your name," he said.

"Aaron." Aaron shut the door. A deadbolt slid into place.

"Her grandmother's very sick," Mike said loudly. "And her mother needs her. I'm not going until I see her."

The door opened again. Aaron still stood defiant. There were lights on in the big room. Toddlers played on the floor. A girl sat crossed-legged, watching TV.

"Just talk to me for a few minutes," Mike said.

Aaron reddened. "Go home, doctor. You don't know anything about her . . . about what she's been through."

"Do you love her?" Mike asked.

Aaron glared. "I told you before."

Mike smiled. "Mellissa and her mother lived with me for a while. She's like family."

Aaron's jaw tensed.

"She's a remarkable young woman," Mike said. "You can't let her throw her life away."

Aaron turned his head to look past him. "She doesn't cry without reason here, doctor. She doesn't dream at night with her hands pounding the headboard anymore."

"Her mother might lose in court without Mellissa's help."

"Her mother wanted to send her away. Now she expects her to come running back home?"

"I'll find her. And I'll take her back. Is that what you're afraid of?"

"I'm afraid of what New Orleans has done to her."

"But she can come back here if she wants," Mike said. "After it's over."

Somewhere, behind the barn, an engine cranked and turned over. Mike could not see a car. He heard a bang from a defective muffler, then an accelerating growl. A vintage, rusted out Willys Jeep lurched down the drive, veering around his car. Thibodeaux was right. She was running.

Mike went to his car but couldn't follow. Both Thibodeaux's car and the Jeep had disappeared. Mike dialed Thibodeaux's cell. Thibodeaux didn't pick up for more than thirty minutes. He gave directions to where they were.

"Two men take her to a restaurant closed up tight. I wait,"

Thibodeaux said. "You get here soon."

The restaurant had rooms for rent — single-occupancy cottages that faced the bay. Light glowed behind a drawn yellow shade in one. Smoke drifted upward from a small pipe on the roof.

"She disappear quick, we wait too long," Thibodeaux said. Mike agreed. Thibodeaux looked in a window and came back to Mike. "She with two men from the commune. She got a suitcase by the bed."

Thibodeaux outlined his plan. There was only one door with single key lock below the doorknob. Entrance would take seconds.

They approached the cottage from the side, crouching as they got near. Thibodeaux positioned Mike to the left. Thibodeaux knocked. There was no movement inside. Still crouching, so he was unseen, Thibodeaux knocked again. No answer. Mike stood and rammed his right shoulder against the door near the lock. He followed Thibodeaux in. The two men from the commune stood near the bed, shielding Mellissa behind them.

AT Thibodeaux fixed his gaze on Mellissa.

"Who are you?" Mellissa said.

"It's me, Mellissa," Mike said, stepping to where she could see him. "Your family needs you."

"Go away!"

"I'm not going without you!"

"I'm better here," she said.

Mike moved closer to Mellissa. "We won't hurt you. You need to come back," he said.

Mellissa ducked and dove between him and Thibodeaux, running out the door. Each of the men propelled forward. The first one knocked Thibodeaux against the wall; his head struck the edge of a table. The second toppled him onto the bed. The man was strong, and Thibodeaux struggled to free one of his arms.

The Willys cranked up with a groan, which faded as Mellissa drove away.

"You got a gun?" the first man asked.

Thibodeaux moaned.

"We're unarmed," Mike said. His assailant released him.

The first man had run outside. He was slashing the tires on Mike's rental car. Mike pushed him to the ground, grabbing the knife and throwing it into the darkness of the shrubbery. Thibodeaux came out the door, his attacker behind him. Thibodeaux turned and delivered a kick to the groin that doubled the man over. Thibodeaux hurried to the rental truck. "Get in," he yelled to Mike.

In seconds Thibodeaux had the truck on the road. There was only one road back to the interstate, with only driveways and dead-end property access roads on the sides.

"You sure she went this way?" Mike asked.

"Ain't no choice."

A light snowfall glittered in the lights of the truck. The four inches of fresh ground cover gave a pewter glow to the landscape and made dark silhouettes of the occasional house or barn they passed.

"That's her," Thibodeaux said. "Them lights too dim for a modern car."

Mellissa sped up as Thibodeaux gained on her. Mike saw the Jeep swerve to the right, clip a mailbox, and veer back onto the road to continue on.

Mike looked to Thibodaux. "Slow down."

"We'll lose her."

The truck's headlights glared on the patch of black ice that covered a slight shallow in the road. At first Mike thought it was a clear area, but it was too reflective for road surface, and when the tires hit the ice, the truck turned ninety degrees. The tires caught the road surface again, sideways, and the truck flipped and rolled three times. The engine screamed as part of the dashboard forced the gearshift into neutral. They were upright again, still plunging forward but much more slowly, until the front end hit the trunk of an oak. Mike smelled fuel.

"Get out," Thibodeaux yelled, pushing on his crumpled door. Then he was trying to crank down the window.

Mike kicked his partially opened door. He moved around the back of the truck to help Thibodeaux. Five feet from the door there was an explosion near the rear of the truck. Flames flashed a glimpse of Thibodeaux half out of the truck window. The blast blew Mike back and he lost his balance. Thibodeaux screamed.

Flames were burning under the truck. Mike got to his feet. He was able to grab Thibodeaux under the arms and squeeze him from the truck. He dragged him to the edge of the road, away from the crackling fire. Another explosion lit up the surrounding tree trunks. The inside of the cab shimmered with flame.

Thibodeaux was hurt. Mike assessed the burns to the right side of his face and his shoulder. Thibodeaux's pant leg was ripped, and he had a gash in his left thigh. Mike removed his T-shirt, tore a patch to tamponade the wound, and then stripped the rest into ties for pressure.

"Is he all right?" Mellissa said.

Mike jumped. He had not heard her, too concentrated to catch the groan of the Willys as she returned. He had never expected to see her again.

"It's nothing," Thibodaux said.

"You need treatment," Mike said.

"We can use the Willys," Mellissa said. "He can stretch out on the back seat."

"Is there a hospital?"

"In Damariscotta. But there's an emergency room in Wiscasset."

Mellissa drove the Willys closer to Thibodeaux, and Mike helped him into the backseat.

The ER was in a strip mall and turned out to be a doc-in-the-box operation, more a first aid station than an equipped trauma facility. The attendant on duty called the doc, who took call from home. He was, at first, willing to treat only by phone until Mike talked to him. Mike kept Mellissa close, and got Thibodeaux into an exam room. The attendant helped Mike get Thibodeaux out of his clothes and under a sheet. Mike brought water.

The ER doc was not a surgeon. Thibodeaux had blistered a little. The doc wanted Thibodeaux to go to the hospital in Portland, but Mike convinced him to dress the thigh wound. He directed treatment of the burn areas where needed, suggesting where to place ointments. He got him to sedate AT; the doc didn't like taking directions, but Mike was firm. Without a license to practice in Maine, he had to negotiate when the doc had strong objections.

"You're going to be okay," Mike said to Thibodeaux. "I feel better you're getting treatment."

Thibodeaux looked at Mike blankly.

"The doc's going to keep you for a while."

The sedation and his pain got to Thibodeaux, and he closed his good eye.

"Take the kid to New Orleans," Thibodeaux said. "I come later, you hear?"

Mellissa was sitting in a plastic-upholstered waiting-room chair. "Come on," Mike said.

She followed with a suspicious look. "Your mother needs you. And her lawyer wants to talk to you about home life with your father."

He asked for her keys and directions to the farm.

"Are you going to force me?" she asked.

"I don't know."

There was no traffic on the roads this time of year. The headlight beams cut into the darkness of the woods on the edge of the two-lane state road. After many miles, Mike turned onto a dirt road.

"Why are we going to the farm?" she asked.

"To get your boyfriend," Mike said.

"Why?"

He slowed for ice spots on the road. Snow on the fields now glowed in the reflection on an almost-full moon – unhindered by clouds.

"Can you get out of Maine?" Mike asked.

"Aaron and I have dreams," she said hesitantly.

"Do you have money?"

"Enough." She sighed. "We like it here."

They were within a few miles of the farm. She looked out into the night.

"I thought you'd come to get me," she said. "To take me back."

"I've changed my mind. I'll take you back only if you want. You make the decision."

Mike drove up the drive to the farm. Lights came on inside the farmhouse before he stopped the car.

Mellissa opened the door and ran into the house through the front door. He turned off the engine, rolled down the window, and waited. It was freezing, but the air had a purity to it. Within a few minutes, she came out with Aaron.

"We're getting out," she said.

"Don't tell me anything more. Are you flying?"

They turned and discussed it. "We'll fly."

"Get your stuff."

In two hours they were at the Portland Airport. As they waited on security, he gave them as much cash as he could spare from his wallet and what he could get from an ATM. They made the last regional flight connection to Bangor.

Thibodeaux was still sleeping in the single hospital bed at the facility. Mike waited for him to awake on his own. The attendant slept on a cot in a back room. The doc had gone home.

Near dawn, Thibodeaux awoke with a start and sat straight up. Within seconds, he knew where he was.

"She got away," Mike said.

"Goddamn it, Boudreaux. How long has it been?"

"Few hours."

Thibodeaux spat on the floor. "It lot of work tracking her down," he said. He stood. "Let's go."

"Maybe the attendant can give you a ride back to your truck. I'll try to make the noon flight back," Mike said.

"No way, man."

"It's the only way. You'll never find them."

Thibodeaux considered his options. But didn't reply.

Mike arrived in New Orleans in the evening. Catherine's lawyer was at the airport to greet the plane.

"What the hell happened?" he asked.

"She got away. She'll come home on her own someday," he said.

"Don't bullshit me, man. I don't need you working against me." The lawyer walked away.

Mike went directly from the airport to Catherine's mother's house to tell Catherine about Mellissa.

"She didn't want to come back to New Orleans," he said.

"I sent you to bring her back. Not to find out what she wants," Catherine said in a tense voice. "I need her."

"She's got a future," Mike said.

"She's not yours, Michael. You have no right to butt in."

He was flooded with sadness. He did not believe he was at fault here.

"We'll talk later," he said. He turned and walked down the concrete path toward his car.

"I'm sorry," she called. "I didn't mean . . ."

He waved. "It's okay," he said. She's not herself. No one can blame her.

CHAPTER 33

The final threats of foreclosure came every few days now. Catherine was numb to them. She recognized official documents without opening the letters, and burned them. She refused to sign for certified mail.

Michael urged her to live in the Quarter with him. She would, someday. But now she was living in the only remnant of her former life. She had come to believe that if she let it go, she would free fall into oblivious destitution. Mike offered her money. Offered to support the house payments until she could settle the divorce. But she knew the strain of money would divide them eventually. He was not wealthy working as a doctor for an institutional salary.

She did not feel confidence that she was attractive anymore. Everything ripe had rotted, everything smooth had eroded, everything moist and healthy had dried up. Life was just dying. But she had her pride in her past, and she believed she might work things out . . . if she could just hold herself together. She had Mike, and she did not want to fracture the only thing she still had of value – their love. She repeatedly refused his money.

She had only the one lawyer now. Others had left for nonpayment. The one remaining was desperate for work, and hoped, as the lone counsel, for a major chunk of any settlement from Clayton. But he was barely competent as a lawyer, much less a domestic relations lawyer. He needed income and stayed on the case even though he thought the accusations of abandonment against her, and her love for another man, had ruined any chance for a significant windfall.

In the midst of her despair, Catherine received a certified check for ten thousand dollars from Mellissa and Aaron. A few weeks later she received another. She did not tell Michael, but she began to hope that some solution was possible. She staved off repossession. She began looking for a job. And for a few minutes each day, she had some hope she'd recover to love Michael as he deserved, and to be a mother to Mellissa.

Over the next few weeks, she saw Clayton at times when she went out for errands. He never approached her, but he did not try to hide. She knew it was ridiculous, but fear gripped her when she saw him. She told herself over and over: Clayton was an accomplished physician with intelligence and skills to help people, and she should be convinced he would not harm her, or any human. She would ignore him.

One night she felt him around the house again – not a sighting, but a spirit mostly conjured in dark and silence – and called the police. They found nothing.

Michael came to her when he could. But with Clayton gone from the surgical staff, the workload at the hospital had increased drastically. She never abandoned their dream of living the rest of their lives together. When a sliver of doubt slipped into her mind, she busied herself with cleaning the stove or refrigerator, or talking to her mother, until it was gone.

Another certified check from Mellissa brought another ten thousand dollars. A yellow Post-It was stuck to the check. "I'm fine. I miss you. Love, M."

Catherine felt an urge to destroy this check. It was incredibly generous. It must come mainly from her boyfriend's reserves. But she fought humiliation. How silly. What kindness. She would not be embarrassed to accept handouts from her daughter; she was grateful for Mellissa and Aaron's generosity. But the reality of foreclosure still loomed. She feared eviction if the balance was not satisfied in full, and she had been using some of Mellissa's money for daily expenses.

She drove to the bank that held the mortgage. She deposited Mellissa's check. She knew the loan officer well by now. She sat in front of his desk.

"Here," she said taking out her checkbook. "What will it take?"

He shrugged. "It's paid up. I think you're current."

"It's impossible."

"Late yesterday, I think. Pearleena took the payment."

"Who paid?" she stammered. "My father?"

"I'll ask." He called and asked Pearleena the details.

"Not your father. A doctor. Boudreaux."

She was confused. She still believed to accept Mike's generosity would eventually destroy his love. She was sure of it. When she was living with him, she had been able to split expenses. But now they were apart, and she had problems far distant from his world and their future. Michael was comfortable in his nonmaterialistic way, but not wealthy, and she could not erode his savings. If they could marry, she would work. She would solve this mess. And she would not be debt-ridden and dependent. It could be different.

She drove to the hospital, only ten minutes away. She paged him and they met in the lobby. He was in scrubs.

"Michael, you can't be paying my mortgage. I don't need it. Mellissa's helping out."

"I can't let you be evicted. What would you do?"

"Please, I can manage. I don't want this changing what we have together."

She tried to write him a check for the payment. It would only cover a small fraction of the total amount he had paid, but he would see she had resources. He refused.

"Oh, Michael," she said. She hugged him, oblivious to the crowd in the lobby. "Don't do anything like this again," she whispered. "I don't want money ever to come between us."

He held her shoulders and looked at her earnestly. "Nothing will ever come between us," he said.

CHAPTER 34

Iris tried to cooperate as Catherine coaxed cubes of beef into her, but she lost concentration and missed the spoon like a newborn. She knocked it out of Catherine's hand, and then her arms jerked up and tilted the tray so that dishes fractured on the hardwood floor.

"That's enough for tonight," Catherine said, and she fought Iris's flailing movements to attach the arm and leg restraints to the side rails.

"It's best," Catherine said with a touch of guilt at restricting her mother. Then she set to cleaning up the mess on the floor.

When she returned, Iris was calm. Catherine sang to soothe her mother. "Irene ... goodnight Irene ... I'll see ... you in ... my dreams." A soft, sad song Iris had sung to her so many years ago.

When Iris babbled, rambled in time, she used enough cleanly wrought details so Catherine knew her meaning. "My mother told me I should never have children!" Iris spat out once, and Catherine thought she had made that up. Iris said she knew her mother had always wanted more grandchildren. And Iris had tried for pregnancy after Catherine, but somehow had gotten her tubes scarred, so new little Irises never made it into the womb. That's what she was told.

Once, Catherine was embarrassed by her mother's honesty when she blurted blasphemies, then breathed deeply to yell. "I hate his breath," Iris screamed. "I hate the touch of his filthy hands," she then whispered.

Catherine had placed her hand on Iris's arm. "Don't touch me," Iris yelled. She was lost in some internal dream. *Maybe she thinks it's Gabe's hand.* "Don't ever touch me again," Iris cawed. "Goddamn you." Then, as was her habit, she dropped into a long period of quiet.

Mike came as often as he could to see Iris and Catherine. Sometimes he watched Iris when Catherine went to get food. At other times he sat with Iris, content to know it seemed to help her. He talked to her about his mother and college. He talked about dreams and nightmares. Sometimes he made her laugh, and when he sometimes made her sad, he quickly changed his line of chatter.

This night, Catherine had made iced tea, and they both sat in chairs by Iris, who was restrained with her eyes closed.

With Mike's help, she had initially tried to prop up a TV on a stand, but the TV agitated Iris and they had taken it out of the room. Mike had brought a radio, and there were some stations that played suitable music. Catherine had tuned in a classical station and a string quartet played at muted volume.

"Is that you, Clayton?" Iris asked.

They thought she had been asleep.

"It's me, Iris. Michael."

"The moon has spots from the crud . . ."

"Mother!"

"It does."

"Try to sleep," Catherine said.

Iris fixed on Mike.

"I love Catherine," he said.

Iris tried to sit up but was held by the restraints. "I cannot think well," she said with absolute clarity.

Catherine gently touched her mother's shoulders, but Iris refused to relax.

"Impeach me," Iris said.

"Release you?" Catherine glanced at Mike.

Iris groaned what seemed to be agreement.

Catherine released the restraints on Iris's arms. Her mother breathed quickly with exhaustion and made no precipitous movements to escape. Catherine released the leg restraints.

For the moment, Iris's attention had lost Catherine.

Iris babbled her jumble of thoughts. She was subdued. She cried. She fell asleep.

"Her wires may be crossed. But she had something on her mind,"

Mike said.

"I'll ask her tomorrow. Sometimes I can understand."

Iris lay on her back now, her arms on her chest, her feet spread. Catherine walked Michael to the door and said goodnight.

The next morning, the alarm clock failed and Catherine slept more than two hours beyond Iris's morning meal. She rushed to her mother's room. The room was silent. The bed empty. The window open.

Iris's nightclothes were draped over a chair, as if she might have been taking a bath and would be back in seconds to put them on. Catherine ran to the window. The body was naked, lying face down in the muck of a storm-drenched flowerbed under the open window, the arms splayed as if she might have tried to soar. She had fallen maybe fifteen feet. She looked discarded. Catherine cried out and hung her head. But she did not weep. When it was obvious her mother was dead, she felt relief that quickly turned to guilt. God, she thought. The restraints. I killed her.

After the body had been removed, she called Michael. The removal of the restraints was not wise, but it was a kindness, Michael had said, and she continually pleaded that to herself. Her mother had savored restful freedom; it was a gift deserved. That was the way she would think about it, always.

Mike saw the obituary photo of Iris in the Sunday paper in the doctors' lounge as he was waiting to start a case; it was an early photo taken when Iris and Gabe had made Catherine Queen of Rex. He quickly read the hollow words about her life, and he wondered if Catherine wrote them herself, or if she'd depended on strangers. But the image of Iris as a strong woman, so different from her later years, grabbed his interest. Her life had turned into an empty, decorated eggshell. Her isolation was hidden in the glitter of her fragile world. A sham marriage. A child whom she would never really let love her. Had she been afraid to accept Catherine's affection, afraid it might diminish her in some way? And it was easy to blame her for Gabe's failures as a husband and a father. She must have fueled at least some of Gabe's evil by her cold ineptness, caring enough only to listen and console.

She was not simply a victim of fate, a log floating on the Mississippi until it reaches the Gulf, where it decays into the elements. Not the Iris he had known, and who had hurt Catherine. She had paddled downstream through life on her own, taking advantage of rapids and falls to catapult her onward, always alone, finally to run aground.

The wake was on Saturday.

Clayton' leg had a complication of infection after his third reparative procedure, and he was walking with a four-pronged cane; he had not been out of the house for two days. His leg still ached where the bullets had shattered part of the tibia and femur. His peers in the hospital had twice placed and replaced rods and pins. He positioned the leg on a stool while sitting, and in the bed he propped it up with pillows. He'd find a position that seemed to help, and then it would start aching again. Then he'd move to a new position. He'd not had a real sleep since Maddie had shot him.

On the third day, the pain was worse when the rain moved in. On the fourth day, the sun was shining and there was a brisk breeze. The pain was less, and he went out to collect the delivered newspapers. He didn't need the cane this day. He sat down to read. He turned to the obituaries.

The obituary for Iris inflamed him. Nothing was accurate. You'd think the woman had been a saint, God's chosen daughter, who gave her life so that others might be saved.

Where was the truth? She had been a bitch. Her husband a cheat. Her daughter a witless whore. Was it Iris's genes that had ruined Mellissa?

There would be a wake. Catherine's fake tears. Mike holding her hand. He could not erase the images that haunted him with incredible detail. He could think of nothing else. He drank bourbon out of a water glass. But the images were still there. He went to bed but could not sleep. He walked until his leg ached more, and then went back to bed. When the sun rose, he loaded his pistol and brewed a pot of coffee to fill a thermos to carry with him on the way to New Orleans.

CHAPTER 35

Iris lay in an open casket at the wake. Her hands were one on top of the other on her chest, the fleshless skin clinging to the bones, as if she'd been dead for months. Her face had a dried-leaf color, with tulip-red lips. There was little relation in this image to her life, except for a maniacal intensity she had taken on in her later years that no embalmer could ever cover up. Most of the mourners looked away after a quick glance, uncomfortable with death, the unskilled preparation, how empty the corpse seemed.

In the reception area, food was laid out on multiple tables and a bar served mixed drinks, beer, and wine. Mike stood next to Catherine when Mellissa walked in alone. Her plain but attractive mauve dress was designed to deemphasize a pregnancy, but she was clearly in the third trimester.

Catherine gasped when she saw Mellissa. A surge of joy surprised her, followed by a confusion as to how she should respond; she feared humiliation in front of former family friends if Mellissa rejected her. Certainly she wouldn't turn away from her.

Mike did not hesitate and stepped quickly to Mellissa, taking her in his arms. Mellissa laughed in delight at seeing him. Many in the crowd were looking now, and there were gasps of recognition.

Catherine watched the affection of Mike and Mellissa, and all her resentments fell from her. She walked over to Mellissa when Mike released her, and she held her tightly. "I love you," she said. "All that you've done."

No one in the room but Mike heard, but everyone in the room sensed some significant emotional transference, and the crowd surged forward to say hello to Mellissa. Mike squeezed Catherine's hand,

and she looked at him, her eyes happier than he had seen them in
many months.

After a few minutes of greetings, Mellissa came back over to
Catherine and Mike.

"When are you due?" Mike asked.

"Eleven weeks." Mellissa paused, and then took Mike's hand.
"Aaron and I wondered if you'd be the godfather. You don't have to be
at the christening. We'd be pleased just to have you say yes."

Mike grinned in surprise and pleasure. They cared for him, and
he was proud of it. "I wouldn't miss it," he said. He hugged Mellissa
again. Catherine smiled. She had already begun to feel the joy of
imagining her role as a grandparent, and she was pleased that Mellissa
was so happy to see her.

Clayton had parked a block away in a grocery store parking lot. He
had flanked the funeral home and approached the rear double door
that opened out into an alley, away from the front entrance where the
mourners entered. He stood in the shadows. One of the doors was
ajar. He could hear the mourners. He saw movement in the parlor
but could not make out faces.

He heard the hushed condolences. Heard Michael's voice.
Michael's joy at Mellissa's return angered him. He heard her voice . . .
happy and confident in ways he never remembered.

Catherine's voice seemed to sing. He'd heard that before, when she
was young, when she had seen life as all hers. He flushed, trembled.
His leg pain shot up through his body into his brain. God how he
hated her.

He hobbled in through the back door.

Mike paused when he saw Clayton. He was barely recognizable,
unshaven for days, his tan chinos stained, his polo shirt torn under
one armpit. His cane supported him, his back hunched over. His
watery eyes moved constantly around the interior, sometimes looking
up without purpose. He carried a gun loosely in his left hand, the
barrel pointing down. Mourners became silent, suddenly aware of his
presence as if an icy mist had engulfed the room.

Catherine saw Clayton. She gasped. Clayton moaned, his face contorted. She reached for her bag that she had placed on a chair next to the wall. She fumbled with a drawstring that closed the top, finally freeing it; she reached in and removed the gun.

"Jezebel . . ." Clayton yelled. He held the gun before him, his head bent, his eyes looking at it as if he were surprised it was there. He raised the gun, aiming as if at a target practice.

Catherine was trying to free the safety on her pistol, her eyes down. It clicked. She never saw Clayton's blazing, rheumy eyes.

Mike leapt forward toward Clayton. In two steps he would be on top of him, coming from the side.

But Clayton fired . . . people fell to the floor . . . others headed for the doors. Catherine held her gun loosely in both hands, working to point it toward Clayton. Suddenly, with the bullets entering her body, her motions turned arbitrary; her gun fell to the floor as she slumped. Mike tackled Clayton on his injured leg. Clayton cried out and went down. Mike tried to rise and Clayton swung the gun at Mike's head, stunning him.

Catherine moaned, lying on her side. Two shots had entered her chest, the third in her left temple. Mike reached her in seconds, felt her heart stop as he held her, felt her last breath on his lips as he saw the absence of the soul cloud her eyes into an opaque stare at some infinitesimal world.

Clayton struggled to stand. He froze, looking at Catherine, his mouth in the grimace of a misdirected smile. He was feeling a surge of murderous power. He focused on Mike, her lover. His anger shifted; he felt the need of the executioner . . . to deliver justice. He positioned his cane, retrieved his gun and aimed, his sight on Mike.

Mellissa, with her hands holding her belly, saw her father's movement. Her mother's gun was on the floor inches from her. She couldn't bend to reach it and she fell to her knees and grabbed it.

The gun arm had sagged as Clayton took aim, but he recovered. The barrel was directly pointed now at Mike. Mellissa's right hand felt the chill of the gun metal and she brought the gun up. She fired twice.

Clayton felt little pain with the first bullet. How odd. His leg pain was gone! An ironic blessing. He crumpled, but it seemed as if he were someone else, not himself. He saw two more movements of the gun in Mellissa's hands, but heard nothing. Then she faded as the scene faded, the edges closing in, the figures of Catherine held by Michael and Mellissa lowering her weapon rapidly diminishing, as if he were in a rocket leaving Earth.

CHAPTER 36

Almost two months after Catherine and Clayton were buried, in separate cemeteries, Mellissa delivered her healthy girl and Mike flew to California. Aaron met him at the airport. Aaron strapped Mike's bag in the bed of his pickup truck. On the driver's-side door was a logo with red letters and a black border: AARON BERNSTEIN, new line, RESTORATIONS, with a phone number below.

Aaron seemed subdued as they drove. He'd said no more than "Hello," and "I'll take your bag."

Aaron maneuvered onto the 101 and kept a strict five miles below the speed limit. Mike remembered him as a confident, talkative kid.

"Where do you live now?" Mike said.

"Not too far."

"You like it here?"

"It's okay."

"Better than Maine?"

"I guess."

There was a snapshot of Catherine holding the baby, Mary Beth, taped to the dashboard.

"A great kid," Mike said.

Aaron smiled grimly.

After an hour, Aaron pulled into the drive of a small white bungalow. The front door opened as they got out of the truck. "Your bag is safe in the back," Aaron said.

A small, wizened woman with gray hair stood in the doorway. She smiled when Mike was close. "I'm Clara Bernstein, Aaron's mother."

Mike held her outstretched hand. "And Mary Beth's grandmother," he smiled. He let go of her hand. "Is this your first grandbaby?"

"Why, yes. It is. She's just beautiful."

The front door opened into a living room with a sofa and a recliner facing a large TV set on a stand. On the left was an open dining area with a door to a small kitchen. A door in the back wall led to a hall, and presumably the bedrooms.

Mellissa sat in the recliner. She was nursing. She held a blanket so her breast and the baby were not visible. "Hi," she said.

"And you. How are things?"

She looked down at the baby, lifting the edge of the blanket.

"I'll finish up in a minute so you can take a look."

Mellissa had gray circles around her eyes. She had put on weight, and her cheeks were full. Her dull eyes moved slowly and seemingly without purpose, the whites reddish and moist as if she'd been crying. Her lips were dry and cracked. She separated the baby from her and discreetly adjusted her bra and buttoned her blouse. She burped the child over her shoulder, and then cradled it in her arm as she tried to stand. She was weak and could barely move; Aaron rushed over to take the baby, and held her up to Mike.

The newborn had sparse black hair matted in clumps and curls. The eyes were shut. The face looked relaxed, but the skin was flushed. On the left side was a red birthmark that covered the cheek, the eye, and the forehead. It would change with time, fade, but there would be a deformity. There was no effective treatment.

Mellissa had turned so she could push herself out of the chair. Once standing, she turned to Mike and fell into his arms. "I'm so glad you came," she whispered. "I've missed you."

He held her, felt her relax in his arms. "My godchild. She's beautiful."

He let her go and she stood back. He reached in his coat pocket and handed her a small box wrapped in white paper and tied with gold ribbon and a bow. She opened it.

"How thoughtful," she said, holding up a silver cross on a chain. She showed it so Mrs. Bernstein could see. "Do you like it, Manna?" But Mrs. Bernstein did not respond, and turned to bring refreshments for them all from the kitchen.

They talked in spurts for a while. Mellissa was still exhausted.

She had had preeclampsia, and had been symptomatic. Aaron's business was in a slump, as the demand for houses had disappeared. Mrs. Bernstein already missed Philadelphia. This was her first trip out West. She had arrived the night before last.

"Aaron," Mike said, "help me with my bag." The two of them went out front. As they got near the truck, Mike touched his arm.

"What's going on?" Mike asked Aaron.

"Nothing. It's Manna, and Mellissa's postpartum depression."

"I understand the depression. What about Manna?"

"She doesn't want the christening. She doesn't want her granddaughter to be brought up Catholic."

"What do you want?"

"I want what Mellissa wants. That's the way I've always wanted it."

"Then that's the way it should be. Do you want me to talk to your mother?"

"I don't think so. She won't change how she feels."

"But she's going to let the christening go on, isn't she?"

"She won't attend. That's what she told us."

"She came all this way . . ."

"She's stubborn."

Mike grabbed him by the shoulders so he could not look away. "Everything's going to be all right. You and me. We're going back in there and make those women happy. Your daughter's christening is a joyous occasion in the witness of the Lord. Let's do it for Mary Beth, and for Mellissa."

He didn't move.

Mike shook him. "Did you hear me?"

Aaron nodded slowly.

The christening went fine, but without Mrs. Bernstein standing by her family. Mike had a picture of his godchild laminated and installed it in his wallet. Back home, Mellissa sent him seven-by-five photos of Mary Beth every few weeks, which he framed and lined up on his mantel. Mellissa called regularly as she regained her health.

CHAPTER 37

More than a year later, after Mass, Mike walked out of the Cathedral. Rosie Dayside walked up to him.

"Girl wants to buy a man a cup of coffee," she said.

She was pretty in a white knee-length dress, a red bow gathering her hair into a ponytail.

They sat near the back of Cafe du Monde and ordered coffee.

"Where's Steven?" he asked.

She looked at him, puzzled. "Who's Steven?"

"Your husband. Works at Pierre's."

"It was Chris. And he worked at the Ritz."

He had to smile.

"You living in the Quarter?" he asked.

"I didn't marry him, Michael."

He was surprised.

"It just didn't seem right," she said.

A tiny Vietnamese woman with a permanent smile delivered coffee.

"It was terrible about Catherine. Are you okay?"

He took a long, slow sip.

"Catherine and I had those talks at the retreat," she said. "I still remember them. I liked her."

"I miss her," he said.

"Was it hard for her?"

"Her mother died. Did you know? Her father abandoned her in every way. And her leaving her husband, and trying to do the best for her daughter, she was filled with guilt and anger that no one should be forced to live through."

"But her daughter's doing well?"

"Has a little girl now. I visit every few months."

"She's happy?"

"I think so, Rosie. How can we know? Aaron, her husband, seems to love her. But I always wonder if Mellissa will ever reach her potential."

"Does she have a career?"

"She helps Aaron. But I meant in love. Catherine loved. At times she was selfless in ways that amazed me."

"Did her daughter know that?"

"She did at the end. I think she realized what her mother had been through."

"But they were not close?"

"I doubt it, except maybe on the last day. Mellissa rebelled, I think because of what she saw at home. She reached out to strangers. And she found a good kid for a husband. In the end, I think she understood that her mother had really needed what she needed, and found."

"Love."

"Real love you didn't doubt and could always depend on."

"What about you, Michael? Have you found someone?"

"Catherine's still with me, Rosie. I still relive the good times in quiet moments." He signaled the waitress for more coffee. "How's your career going? I saw photos of your work on the back of the symphony program. Your new exhibit."

"I'm moving to New York," she said.

He was surprised.

"Two galleries have been selling my work. The sculptures especially. It's where I want to be. I hope to rent a studio in Brooklyn."

Fresh coffee arrived. He settled the bill.

"That's terrific," he said. *My God, she's leaving.*

"Come visit," she said. "It'll be a few months. But I've got a chance of a couple pieces being accepted in an exhibit on American art at the Whitney."

"You've come a long way," he said.

She didn't understand.

"With your career."

She smiled. "Still not definite. But no matter what happens about the move, we could take a few days in New York and you could come see the galleries that are carrying me. They do it first class."

He looked up. She was staring at him. "That would be great," he said. He'd said it by reflex, but as he held her gaze, he knew it would be possible with time. And he knew he would enjoy it, the trip . . . and being with Rosie. *She's one in a million.*

Books by William H. Coles

McDowell
Creating Literary Stories: A Guide for Fiction Writers
Illustrated Short Fiction of William H. Coles 2000–2016
Short Fiction of William H. Coles 2000–2016
The Surgeon's Wife
The Spirit of Want
Sister Carrie
Facing Grace with Gloria and Other Stories
The Necklace and Other Stories
Story in Literary Fiction: A Manual for Writers
Literary Fiction as an Art Form: A Text for Writers
The Short Fiction of William H. Coles 2001–2011
The Illustrated Fiction of William H. Coles 2000–2012

storyinliteraryfiction.com

CPSIA information can be obtained
at www.ICGtesting.com
Printed in the USA
LVHW040417040820
662291LV00006B/462

9 780997 672947